I hope you enjoy

David A. Wright

RIVER ROCK

BY

DAVID A. WRIGHT

xulon PRESS

ACKNOWLEDGEMENT

I'm one of those people whose family and friends are loaded with talent, and I have tapped into just about all of their talents to bring this book to fruition. I could not have done it without everyone's encouragement, support and help.

To my children Karen Shelton (who helped edit), Ted Wright, Melissa Keeton and Kristi Baird, who all read and gave their input into the book, listened to me, and encouraged me; thank you. A special thank you goes to my niece, Barbara Sue Makamson, for her many hours of help and encouragement. My son-in-law Brian Baird worked countless hours reading and editing again, and giving me good advice all along the way. Thank you Brian. And to a very talented friend and author, Diana Gill, thanks for taking your valuable time to read and critique my writings.

Rick Bragg, an author whose writings I appreciate and admire, once gave me a written promise to buy my book. For his inspiration I am thankful.

My big brother, Stanley, when asked what he thought about his little brother writing a book replied "I didn't even know he could read – much less write!" Someone please read this to him and explain that no, it's not about him.

I could write a complete book on my most ardent supporter, my best friend and wife, Sandy. Thank you Sandy for telling me I could do this! And above all, thank you God for giving me "just what I needed when I needed it".

DEDICATION
ॐ

To My Grandchildren

Molly

Christopher

Emily

Katherine

Austin

Alex

Jacob

Ian

Samuel

PROLOGUE

୬୨

As the river flows and bends through the Mississippi Delta during the heavy rains of the spring or the slow lumbering slide of summer, it shapes its path and the people along its banks.

Like the river's constant current shapes a rock, so the people are shaped by life's currents. These residents along the Mississippi Delta, no matter what their ancestry, struggle to make a living. And through their struggles, they have become strong.

Even now as the Mississippi flows, their lives have become stronger and more solid - just as solid as the river rock itself.

As our lives flow along, we sometimes feel the lure to return to the place of our youth, to the people who were nearest and dearest to our hearts. We may long to recall the places and events of our lives, even the dialect: all the things that made us become who we now are.

We carry these places, people and events in our memory, and perhaps – just perhaps – we might someday find answers to unanswered questions. And in doing so, we may come to realize just how our own lives were shaped.

Chapter 1

ॐ

All six foot two of Jake Southern stepped out of his rental car onto the gravel-covered road atop the levy, giving him a view of one side of the winding big river, and on the other, the summer haze-covered landscape of the Mississippi Delta. Jake was slim, muscular, and tanned with graying temples, and he had come home again.

Leaning against the car, he couldn't help but think back to his boyhood long ago. Twenty-five years? He was seventeen, living in the old tow boat his dad had partially restored long before he was born, before his dad went off to the Korean War. Jake could remember the day his ill father, rode away in the Judge's big, black car to the hospital in Jackson, never to return. He could vividly recall the look, as he turned to see his mother, tired and weary, and that look still hurt deep inside him even now. At one time she had been a southern beauty, but on that day, she was simply frail and worn.

A few weeks later, the Judge drove up to the old boat, alone, to break the news that his dad had died. Soon after, his mom would be gone; most folks said she died of a broken heart. Jake's thoughts wandered back to his youth;

"You better hurra up wit dat grass cutt'en. Da Judge ain't pay'en you, till you is finish!"

"Dat boy, u is gotta stay on him all da time", Della complained as she turned in disgust and looked at Jessie who was watering the flowers around the porch.

Della and Jessie had been with Judge Nathan B. Cole as long as Jake could remember. It was as if the judge were a guest in that big old rambling house and Della and Jessie were the owners. Della, with her strong will, would always hide her kind heart behind her grumbling and complaining.

Like the time Jake had a head cold. He fondly remembered looking out the porthole of the boat seeing Della lead the way while Jessie followed. Through the mud and gravel road, they came to the river, up the bending planks and onto the tow boat to prepare her old brown sack full of long remembered family remedies for croup, colds, flu and the like. She came fussing all the way. "I don't have time to bury no ugly, little, skinny white boy."

All the while, Jessie was smiling with his kind natured smile, doing Della's bidding, even though Jake knew that this gentle man had the power and strength of five men.

"De Judge say you better mind me" she had said. "Now put this poultice on and quit yo fuss'in!"

Jake and Jessie had talked on one of their many fishing trips about the first time he and Della had laid eyes on Judge Cole.

It was an early, warm, fall day and young Nathan had skipped school; and as a lot of young men in the post World War II days, he began to have wanderlust. On this particular day just outside town, Jessie and Della were standing near a large glass water jug, wrapped in wet burlap to keep it cool, when this young white boy walked up and asked, "Mind if

I have a drink?" Startled, Jessie turned to the boy, not realizing he was there.

"We ain't got but one dipper!"

"That's fine with me!" the boy replied, and reached for the metal dipper that was hanging by a wire on the side of the jug.

Unscrewing the lid, young Nathan plunged the dipper into the refreshing water. Raising the dipper to his lips, he made a gulping sound as he drank, and the clear, cool water ran down the sides of his mouth.

Jessie and Della found this unusual because white folks didn't drink after coloreds.

"What's wrong with dis child?" Della thought.

Reaching out his hand, he said with a grin, "My name's Nathan Cole! What's yours?"

Jessie was caught off guard but reached for young Nathan's hand and was surprised by the boy's firm grip.

"Day calls me Jessie and dis girl, she Della!"

Della stepped forward and spoke up, disregarding the boys outreached hand. "What you do'en way out here boy, in all dis heat?"

"I'm kinda playing hooky from school and thought I'd take a walk in the country, but I didn't realize it would get so hot this time of year."

"Who y'all pick'en for?" Nathan thought it might be a good idea to change the subject.

"Dis heres Mr. Hacket's place!" Jessie spoke up, "We is pick'en for him!"

"I wouldn't want your job in this heat!"

Della glared, "Guess you ain't got to have a job, is you?"

"I don't suppose I do!" Nathan's mind raced for a quick idea to show this girl that he wasn't a rich white kid, and that he wasn't afraid of hard work.

"I'll tell you what, I'll pick cotton the rest of the day and you can have whatever I pick!"

Della looked surprised and said, "Sounds fine wit me! Dere a sack is, at da end of dat row."

Nathan walked over and lifted the nine-foot, tar-bottom sack, placed the strap over his head, and then around his neck.

Jessie asked as he led the way, "Is you ever picked?"

"No but it doesn't look that hard."

Jessie just smiled knowingly and told the boy, "I'll show you how hits done."

The tall young black man began reaching into the stalks for the puffs of cotton, as he bent over. Nathan followed, watching as Jessie showed him the 'fine art of cotton picking', as Nathan would fondly recall the backbreaking, hot, hand scarring experience.

At the end of the day, Della was impressed with this white city boy, and the truth was, she was most impressed when he didn't hesitate to drink out of the dipper.

"How long has the Judge been in my life", Jake thought? Judge Cole was a war hero, politician, fisherman, gambler, hunter, and a lover of refined southern women; a believer in swift justice, and God.

Jake's memory flashed back to a hot summer afternoon in his youth. He recalled slipping into the courtroom just to get out of the heat. He was also interested in all the commotion surrounding the arrest and trial of a local thug, who had been charged with beating his wife while in a drunken stupor.

There they sat: Bo Jenkins for once sober, with his sneaky lawyer Twill sitting beside him. Across the room sat Bo's wife, Rose Lee. Her eyes were blackened and her nose bandaged. She sat looking down at the floor seemingly ashamed of what had happened to her.

Without warning Bo jumped onto the table, grabbed Twill's pen, and lunged toward Rose Lee, swearing that he was going to get her for sure this time.

A great thunder erupted in the courtroom, and Bo fell to the floor, a large hole in his temple. The Judge stood above them all with a 357 Magnum, still smoking in his hand as he bellowed, "Twill, you owe this court $25 for contempt. Bo you are guilty as charged. This court is dismissed!"

That was the Judge quick, firm and just.

And now here Jake was once again, in a place that at times he thought he would never see again. The heat of summer still stuck to his skin, as he remembered the hot summer nights when no breezes blew and the hum of mosquitoes were a constant companion. It was not a lot different from other places in the world he had been, except for the smell. Here it was the smell of cotton bolls - not the smell of death and decay.

One week ago Jake had been standing, watching his unit pass in review; his last day in the army, his retirement parade.

Jake had watched as the young soldiers - smarter, stronger, younger men marched by. Four years at West Point, top of his class, twenty-one year's military service as a soldier's soldier; a down-in-the-dirt, mud, grime and blood of battle soldier, he had been. Now, he had chosen to end his career, an adventure like no other. But peacetime was here. There was no place for old war horses.

Now there was too much politics, leaders advancing in the ranks with suggestion pads and Officer's club parties, and what senators you could impress. This wasn't Jake's Army. Now, he felt, was the time to put all this behind. But what would be ahead?

After the parade Jake stood around and talked with two of his dear friends. Both were 1st Sergeants with chests covered with metals. They reminisced about their first patrol - when they were brand new privates and Jake a fresh West Point butter bar Lieutenant. They recalled how scared they were and how confident Jake seemed with his soft southern accent and confident manner.

"Hell, we just got here", he had reassured them, "I'm not going to let us die yet."

While the three men were reminiscing, a young female soldier approached with a note in her hand, saluted Jake, and reported, "Colonel Southern, this call came for you today, sir."

Jake returned the salute and thanked her, glancing at the two sergeants who were watching the young woman as she walked away.

One of the sergeants commented, "You wouldn't know she's a woman in that camouflaged uniform, hat and boots would you?"

Jake smiled as he opened the note. It read:

You get down here, now! We need you.

Della

That was all. Jake knew from whom it came and where it meant for him to "get".

Why not go back home awhile? He had planned to leave for Hawaii and get in some great fishing, but that could wait a while longer. He had felt the lure of the South before, smelled the smells in his sleep, reflected on his boyhood over and over, and now he was being called to go home, this time by a message from Della!

Chapter 2

ॐ

J ake pulled down the long drive to the great, old rambling house, built in the 1800s by some long ago ancestor in the Cole family line.

This was a house that Hollywood could use in some movie to depict a typical affluent plantation home: with six tall white columns across the front and the long porches stretching from one end to the other; with tall wide windows from floor to ceiling that, when opened in the warm summer, would allow a cool breeze to flow through.

Jessie was coming around the garage, straight and powerful, with that gentle smile, though his hair was thinner and grayer. He still appeared to have all the warmth and friendliness that had been there many years ago.

As Jake got out of the car, Jessie strolled up to him. "You ain't skinny no mo boy; you is a fine lookin man. Sho good seein' you!"

"Thanks Jess! How's that mean Della?"

"She da same, just meaner." They both laughed and slapped each other on the back.

There standing on the porch, with a cigar in one hand and bourbon in the other, was the great Judge Nathan B. Cole, with his rumpled blue seersucker suit, tie loosened, white hair - ever portraying the laid back, refined southern gentleman.

"Come on up here son," the Judge motioned to a big white rocker with his cigar.

As Jake approached and shook his hand, he felt, for some reason a strong urge to hug this old friend, but the Judge pulled away clearing his shaky voice.

The screen door opened and out stepped Della in all her glory, though somewhat bigger than he remembered. She was as neat as a pin with her still dark hair pulled back in a bun. She walked over to the two men and gave Jake a frown. "Lord almighty! I don't care if you is grown, I'm gonna let you hug me!"

Jake got up from the rocker and wrapped his arms around her and kissed her honey brown cheek.

"Della!" "You eating your own cooking?"

"Well hit ain't kilt da Judge and Jessie, and hit might do you some good!"

Leaning back from Jake's grasp Della looked into his eyes. "Child, you is come from a long, long way! But you is home now! Praise da Lord!"

"Is you comen to supper?"

The Judge spoke up, "You'll get to feed him Della, he'll be here for awhile I'm sure."

Jake assured her, "I wouldn't miss one of your meals for the world Miss Della."

She turned to open the door. "I wants to talk to you when you gets a chance young man."

Glancing at Jessie, she added, "Come on in here and help me."

"Yes ma'am" Jessie replied.

Stepping thru the doorway behind Jessie, Della looked back. "You is done got to be a fine pretty strapp'en man, Jake Southern!"

When the two left the Judge and Jake on the porch, both men settled back into the big rocking chairs.

"I've been keeping up with you, son, (the Judge always called him son, not Jake, not boy, just son). Glad to see that damn old medal did you some good."

"It was the Medal of Honor, sir" - the highest award any soldier could ever receive for bravery on the battlefield.

Nathan Buford Cole was a Medal of Honor recipient and all the privileges that go with it; one being able to nominate a candidate to the U.S. military academy.

Jake could still remember the day, after his high school graduation, when the Judge walked up to him as he stood at his father's and mother's graves and handed him the medal and a bus ticket to West Point with the simple instructions, "take this medal to the commandant at The Point along with this sealed envelope."

Judge Cole had taken care of all the applications for the appointment.

"Yes sir, Judge . . . it did some good, I think."

The Judge nodded, "I agree."

He sat quietly for a few moments. Then in a soft voice, quieter than his usual booming voice, the Judge said, "Your friend Harley has gotten himself some problems."

"Judge, I'm sorry to say, and you well know, I haven't stayed in touch with anyone since I went away. You've lost me, what's going on with Harley? What trouble?"

Taking the cigar out of his mouth and clearing his throat, the judge leaned back in his chair, "we, well, I mean the town, has kept up with you."

"The Army ran a press release about you retiring, which occurred the same time your old buddy Harley got into his problems. I assumed you would be interested and might want to visit us and maybe give him a hand. Della and I were talking and decided to give you a call. Actually Della insisted and took it on herself."

"It seems that the boy shot some redneck in a fuss over a girl, at Lilly's bar. The local DA, Twill, has got his foot into state politics and is trying to make a name for himself by prosecuting him. He charged the boy with murder one and they've held him without bail, or otherwise his folks would have had him out by now."

"These are the facts as recounted in the newspapers and on TV."

"I'm the presiding judge, therefore all I'm allowed to say about it is, between you and me, he may need your help."

Harley Medler, III, son of the old south - old money, upper class son, grandson, and great grandson of old money and a lifelong friend. He always had a big smile, generous heart, and a fun loving nature.

Jake's mind raced back to his youth to the time Harley pulled up in a cloud of dust in that big, square Lincoln convertible.

"Hey Jake", he hollered as Jake put down his fishing pole, "you still selling that rot gut moonshine for a dollar a half pint?"

"Yeah, but since you got all that money, it will be two dollars for you."

Harley smiled as he walked up the plank of the towboat and took a seat.

"You go'en to the prom tonight?"

"Nope, ain't got the duds."

"Jake, you never have been a fashion statement, with the same old jeans and t-shirt. Didn't think you had any formal clothes, so I brought you some. We're gonna make you look like a prince going to the ball."

They had both laughed and grabbed a fishing pole.

Jake could hear the Judge speaking and begged his pardon for daydreaming.

"You going to church with me today?"

The Judge was a devout Baptist and never missed a Sunday.

"That's right this is Sunday", Jake remembered. "Sure Judge."

Some church members found him somewhat improper. "That man sits in church on Sunday and then sits on that porch drinking bourbon during the week," was sometimes whispered by some of the more "proper" members. But he was in church every Sunday, and if anybody trusted and loved the Lord it was Judge Nathan B. Cole.

Jake recalled the judge saying, "You get real close to the Lord in a fox hole with shells exploding all around, thinking the next one is going to land on top of you - mighty close to the Lord."

As they pulled up to the First Baptist Church, Jake could tell the congregation had grown since he had been away.

He walked beside the Judge and they approached a group of men standing outside. Everyone spoke to the Judge, and he turned and introduced Jake, almost as a proud father showing off his prodigal son.

Standing alone to one side of the steps leading to the church doors was Mr. Harley Medler Jr. and his wife Miss

Anna. Between them was Mr. Harley Medler, Senior, the family patriarch. All had a troubled look on their faces as the Judge spoke. "Fine day we are having folks!" politely nodding to Miss Anna.

The Judge turned to Jake and said, "Go on and visit son. I'll be inside."

Miss Anna spoke first, "It's so nice to see you again Jake."

Sure, Jake thought, poor white trash is what he remembered her calling him to Harley III while he waited in the car prom night. Her exact words as he recalled were,

"Son, why do you hang around with that poor white trash?"

Miss Anna liked to play the rich southern lady to the hilt - proper clothes, proper schools, proper friends; the old, rich southern class system. The help always goes to the back door.

"Thank you ma'am."

"When did you get back in town?" Harley Sr. asked.

"Just today sir."

"Are you staying for good?"

"No sir, just for a visit."

Old Mr. Harley Sr. smiled, "We read about you in the papers. The Judge probably makes them print most of it."

"Heard Harley has some troubles" Jake said, as he thought he might as well get it out in the open.

Miss Anna spoke up, "We have a lawyer from Memphis coming down to take the case. It's just some terrible misunderstanding!"

"Have you seen or spoken to Harley yet?"

"No. I'm going over to the courthouse after church."

The choir could be heard beginning to sing, and everyone started toward the door. Jake went inside and sat down beside the Judge. The sermon that day was about Christ's love.

Jake was thinking, as the preacher spoke, that he had never thought much about the subject of love before, having spent his youth mostly alone.

Except for the Judge, Della, Jessie, Harley III and his career, he had never taken the time to think about love at all. It wasn't that he didn't think he was capable, he just never had time, except maybe those brief visits to Tudo street in Saigon.

"No," he thought, "Seven dollars didn't buy love. And besides, that's not the kind of love the preacher was talking about anyway."

Chapter 3

Af ter church they rode downtown to the courthouse.
The Judge parked the car and turned to Jake, "You
tell the deputy on duty I sent you to talk with that boy. I've
got some paperwork to do in my office."

Stepping from the car, Jake could see the grand old courthouse sitting in the middle of the court square still looking
just as it had in his youth. The courthouse had great white
columns on all four corners, and on the north and south sides,
high in the arches were clocks which chimed out the hours
to be heard all over the small, Mississippi town. At the main
entrance there stood a pedestal holding a granite statue of a
Confederate soldier.

This old building housed not only the courtroom and judge's chambers on the second floor, but on the first floor there were the city and county administration offices.

In the basement were the sheriff's office and jail cells. As a young boy the most memorable thing about the old building was how cool the granite floor felt on bare feet on a hot summer day.

Jake approached the jailer at the desk. The jailer looked up from his newspaper. Jake remembered the face, Deputy Dan Williams. "Figured a bootlegger would have shot you by now", Jake said with a laugh.

The deputy looked up at this tall man, but Jake could see he didn't recognize him. "I'm Jake Southern."

The old deputy's eyes widened and a grin appeared.

"I would have locked you up back when you was sell'en whiskey if that moonshine you was sell'en had been bad. That, and if the Judge woulda let me,"

Back when the state was "dry" as it was called, no liquor was sold legally. However, homemade or moonshine corn whiskey was bought and sold in out-of-the-way places by bootleggers. Their location was passed by word of mouth.

Jake, as a young boy, had gotten into the business as a bootlegger through an old black man named Uncle Ned, who was a fishing friend, and who knew Jake needed money to survive after his parents' deaths.

Jake had brought up the idea of selling whiskey one summer evening to Uncle Ned as they sat on the bank of the river fishing and watching the end of a summer afternoon and the sun set lazily over the river.

"Uncle Ned, I want to sell shine for you!"

"What? Boy, you know you ken go to jail for dat" Uncle Ned answered uneasily.

"I know that but I'd be grateful to you. There are some things I need to do and I need the money."

"You makes enough wit yo worken around town and hepp'in Jessie around da Judge's. What you needs mo money for? Ain't dat enough?"

"Sides dat, you knows dat Deputy Williams, he don't like my peoples anyway, and if he finds my whiskey wit you, he gonna know hits mine."

"I'll tell him I got it from some man from Tennessee. He won't know the difference," Jake pleaded.

Uncle Ned was quiet for a while and reluctantly spoke.

"Jake, you a friend and I trust you. I'z gonna try you for a while, but Lord don't ever let Della know!"

Jake returned to the moment realizing the deputy was talking to him, "I'll bet you're here to see that rich friend of yours, the Medler boy. Man, he seems to be in a big mess of trouble!"

"Yes sir Mr. Williams, I'm here to see Harley."

Deputy Williams turned to get the keys in a box on the wall.

They passed through a series of iron doors and approached the end of a hall. The deputy opened the door to a corner cell. There, lying on a cot with his arms propped behind his head, was Harley.

A smile came to Harley's face as soon as saw his old friend walk into the cell. He rose and grabbed Jake's hand and shook it with a big grin

"Sit down man. Anybody that's been all the places I've read that you've been has got to be tired."

The years had changed Harley some. He seemed taller and had put on a few pounds, his hair was gray. But that smile – that smile was still there.

"What's all this about Harley?" Jake motioned around the cell.

Harley patted the cot next to him inviting Jake to sit down.

Deputy Williams closed and locked the cell door.

"Holler when you want out."

"Thank you sir", Jake responded.

Harley began, "There are a lot of things that have happened since you left Jake. I guess the best place to start is about that time, before you left. Remember the night of the prom?"

Jake nodded.

"That was the night I fell in love."

Jake looked at Harley with surprise. Jake thought he knew everything about his friend in those days.

"With who?"

"With Debbie Jenkins. You know, she's Rose Lee and Bo Jenkins' daughter. You remember Bo, he's the one the Judge shot in court year's ago?"

Jake remembered the day well.

Harley continued on, "Anyway, I've been in love with Debbie all these years. But you know how my folks were when we were growing up. Well they haven't changed any, and they've done everything in the world to keep us apart. Now I've helped them along."

"Harley, what happened? How did you wind up here?" Jake said, looking around the cell.

"I had been out of town on bank business for Dad and was on my way home when I stopped off at Lilly's, where Debbie works. You remember the place, it's been around forever. Anyway, she's been working there for years. I've tried to get her to quit through the years and let me take care of her and our son."

"What son?"

"Told you a lot has happened! Debbie and I had a son. Well, she has a son, and I'm pretty sure he's mine. At least I think so. She's never said so to me, and she's never asked for a nickel of support. I guess she has this pride thing."

"Well, the place was closing up, but these two old boys were still there sitting at the bar grabbing at Debbie and making lude comments. I got into it with them. I asked them to cut it out, and the next thing I knew I was knocked out cold, and when I woke up one of them was dead. The sheriff was standing over me. I heard someone say the man had been shot."

"Did you have a gun with you?" Jake asked.

"There was one on the floor when I came too, but it wasn't mine. I don't even own a gun."

"Jake, you knew me. I haven't changed much. I still grin or talk my way out of trouble."

"Was there anyone else there?"

"No the manager had left Debbie to close up".

"Your mom says they have a lawyer coming from Memphis. He should be here tomorrow."

"Dad came by and told me."

Harley looked at the floor and quietly asked, "Jake, find out if Debbie is okay for me, would you?"

Jake patted Harley on the back, "Okay buddy I'll take care of it, and quit worrying. Is there anything else you need me to do?"

Harley grinned his familiar old grin that Jake remembered so well.

"Yep, I want to be setting on that old tow boat of yours fishing and talking the hours away, like we used to do."

Jake looked into his friend's eyes and put his hand on Harley's shoulder and squeezed it. "Harley, I've been looking forward to that fishing trip for years."

Then Jake turned and called for the deputy to let him out.

As Jake walked through the courthouse, every step on the marble floor seemed to echo throughout the building. He walked to the Judge's chambers and found the Judge leaned back in his old, brown leather chair looking through some papers.

"How's the boy?" the Judge asked looking up.

"Okay, I guess" Jake replied. He looked around at the shelves filled with books and photos on the walls. In the corner was a photo of the Judge as a young man receiving the Medal of Honor from General Douglas McArthur. Jake had always wondered about that medal. Another photo was of Jake's mom and dad on their wedding day, and there was an old newspaper photo of Jake at his West Point graduation. On the desk was a picture of Della and Jessie.

"Sit down son", the Judge motioned to a chair in front of his desk.

"How was your friend? Are you going to stick around and see if you can help him out?"

Jake answered "Sure I will, but what can I do? Sir, I've been gone a long time."

The Judge looked at Jake,

"Jake, you knew everyone around these parts from the high to the low."

Jake interrupted, "But Judge that was twenty-five years ago!"

"Well, there are some folks still around that you knew. This is all too cut and dried in my opinion, and besides, Twill is going to do everything to prosecute, trying to get that State Attorney General spot. And not much makes the headlines better in this state than an old southern rich boy being sent to jail. Twill will milk it for all it's worth and drag the whole family in the dirt. The Meddlers' are the money backbone of this county, and no matter what anybody thinks, I'm concerned about the people of this county. I want that boy to get a fair shake. Come on, I got something for you," the Judge said as he rose from his chair.

Jake peered out the window of the Judge's car at Main Street as they drove along. He couldn't help but notice most of the stores seemed to be out of business and vacant. The streets were filled with potholes, and everything looked more run down than he remembered.

The car started up the levee and over the top. There below, where once had been one of the South's busiest river ports and riverboat building ports, were abandoned workshops and a few boats tied to the marina. At the end of the marina, Jake's eye caught sight of something familiar, his old towboat, floating with a new coat of paint, glistening in the sun.

As they got out of the car and walked down the floating marina, Jake could feel the sway of the ramp with every step. This felt so familiar and right to him.

"Jessie and I fixed her up right after you went to the Point and have kept her up. We thought you would come back home someday. She's like new from top to bottom, inside and out. We couldn't get you to leave that damn old boat when you were a boy after your folk's died. Never did know what you saw in her. All your mom's stuff is still inside."

Jake's hand rubbed the rail of the old boat as he walked inside. Just like the Judge had said, over to one side he saw his mother's rocker and on a small table was his mother's tattered old Bible.

"Now you know you can stay up at the house with us if you want," said the Judge. And Della wants you to come to supper tonight you know."

"If you don't mind Judge, I'd like to stay here now. Tell Della I'll come in the next day or two, but I'm just tired. I grabbed a burger in town earlier."

The Judge smiled, "She's still yours son. Jess and I just fixed her up to get away from Della for awhile."

He laughed as he turned to leave, "I'll get Jessie to bring your car to you in the morning."

Jake went around and opened all the portholes on the old boat to get some breeze from the river, and suddenly realized the effects of the day. He was really tired.

He fell across the bunk onto one of his mother's quilts and began to doze off, relaxing with the slow, gentle rocking of the boat. He was home!

Chapter 4

ૹ

"Wake up son," Jake could feel the soft nudge of his mother's hand as she sat on the edge of the bed. He could hear his father already up and sanding on the outside of the boat.

"How's Daddy today, Mom?"

"He's fine. He's working on this old boat," she said shaking her head.

Melissa Southern had just finished her night shift at the hospital and would get a couple hours of sleep before going to the truck stop where she worked as a waitress, and then back to the hospital again; a never ending cycle.

Young Jake eased out of bed and went topside, where his dad was slowly rubbing sandpaper on a rusted spot. Jake grabbed a strip of sandpaper and placed it on a block of wood and began rubbing as he spoke to his father.

"Good morning, Daddy!"

His father looked down at him and smiled.

"Good morning son!"

Jacob Southern had drifted from job to job after returning from Korea. He had always been a hard worker, but a loner. That is, except when he met Melissa, a young student nurse at the time. Their marriage had been great, full of plans and dreams.

But soon, he went off to war.

After the war, even though he was home, the midnight dreams still hit, the screams in mid-sleep, and the unending restlessness. His eyes would fill with tears, at what seemed a reflection on some distant tragic experience. Melissa would often find him alone in the corner of a dark room balled up. He begged her never to speak to anyone about his condition.

Many nights he would awaken and hold onto her as though she was his life raft in the raging sea of his mind.

"It's time for you to wake up, boy!"

Jake opened his eyes and could see the large black man standing over him. It was Jessie.

"What time is it, Jessie?"

"Hits 10:00 am. You bout slept da day away", Jessie smiled.

"That's the longest I've slept in years", he yawned as he sat up on the cot.

"Sit down Jessie." Jake pointed to a chair beside the bed.

Jessie eased down in the chair.

"We didn't get much of a chance to talk at the house yesterday", Jake began.

"What's going on around town? Everything seems to be drying up."

Jessie, the quiet giant, Jake liked to call him, was a man of few words. But during Jake's youth he had been able to get him to talk, whether it was telling Jake how to fix up an old pickup or explain how a locust makes the noise with their legs. Jessie had always had a patient way about him and knew how to explain things.

"Folks is just mov'in away", Jessie began.

"Guess dy is tired of dis hot country, but most of all day jus ain't no jobs no mo. Since day got dem big machines to do all da farm work. Folks ain't got no way to make a liv'en."

"What about the boat builders? Where are they?"

"I heard da Judge talk'en to some folks on da porch. Dat all dis land was took back by the bank and day has to move. Don't know who its sold to or what fer."

Jake thought this was strange. He remembered talk long ago that this property along the river belonged to the town.

"O yeah", Jessie jumped up with a start, "you is spose to meet some lawyer from Memphis dat's drivin down today. Da Judge say to give you dis," and Jessie handed Jake a piece of paper. It said, T. J. Allison - Half Way Truck Stop at 11:00 am.

Jake dropped Jessie off at the Judges' house and floored his rental car toward the truck stop out on the highway, where his mom had once worked.

As he pulled into the parking lot, he could see most of the dinner crowd was there. He knew the type of crowd. There would not only be truck drivers, but farmers, mechanics, factory workers; a mixture of plain working folks. The same as it had been years ago.

Getting out of the car, he thought to himself, "let me find Harley's pin-headed lawyer and see what I can do for him and get this over with."

Miss Dianne White was sitting at the cash register barking orders to the cook as Jake walked into the dining room. Jake looked at her and smiled.

"Jake Southern! My lord boy, I'd know you anywhere, anytime!" Dianne said as she leaped from her stool and hugged him. She had been his mom's best friend for years.

"You still look just like your momma. The Judge comes by and tells everybody all about you and what war you are fighting in. Did you come home to start one here?" she said with a big smile.

"No, Miss White, I'm looking for a lawyer. Have you got one? He's suppose to be coming from Memphis" Jake said.

"Honey, we got some of everything here, just look around," Dianne said with a wave of her hand.

Jake walked over to two men in suits and asked, "either of you T. J. Allison?" Both shook their heads no.

Jake felt a tap on his arm and turned around.

"Mr. Southern?" he heard as he turned. There at the table was a red-headed, slim figured woman, somewhere in her 40's, dressed in a business suit.

Jake thought "what a knock out!"

"Are you with Mr. Allison?"

"No" she replied, "I am Tenna J. Allison."

"I'm sorry. Mind if I sit? The T. J. threw me off."

Looking up at this tanned, tall, interesting man, she was impressed. After two loser husbands and who knows how many dead-end relationships, it took a lot these days to impress T. J. Allison. "Please do!"

The only ring she could see on his finger was a class ring. Where was it from? My- my West Point. Looks and brains too, she thought.

"I spoke to the Judge last night about seeing my client and he suggested I meet you first," she said. "What do you know about the case?"

"Well, ma'amm" Jake started.

"T. J." she interrupted.

"T. J., I just got back in town yesterday and went by to see Harley. He told me his version of what happened, and quite frankly I don't think he would shoot anyone."

"Well, Mr. Medlers' family has given me carte blanche to get this mess cleared up. They felt an out-of-town attorney would do the most good, and I am licensed in Mississippi."

Jake thought, "Wonder what carte blanche costs these days?"

"Her eyes", he thought and then shook himself. "What in the world is wrong with me?"

"T. J." he continued, "Would you like to go over to the jail?"

"That would be wonderful, thank you," she replied, and put some money on the table from her purse.

As they walked toward the door, Miss White hollered, "Jake, come on back when you find the time, so I can feed you." He saw her warm smile and wave.

"You can follow me downtown T.J., I'm in the blue sedan."

"Sounds good to me!"

Jake looked in his rearview mirror and could see T.J. behind him with her sunglasses on.

She looks good even from a distance and thru a windshield, he thought. They pulled up to the jail door, behind the courthouse, and got out.

"I'll wait outside", Jake said as he approached her.

She nodded and went inside.

About the time Jake was turning away, Deputy Williams appeared from the door, looking backwards as he walked out.

"Damn fine looking woman" he murmured as he walked toward Jake.

"Hi Deputy" Jake said.

He looked at Jake and grinned, "I'm old son, but I can still see. And I liked what I saw". Jake smiled in understanding.

"Mr. Williams has anyone seen Debbie Jenkins since the shooting? I have some things I would like to talk to her about."

"Naw, guess she blew town. Probably didn't want to be involved."

"Has anybody tried to find her?"

"Son, we do the best we can do, but we don't have the manpower to go looking all over for some gal that works in a beer joint."

"It was all pretty cut-and-dried. There was a fight, and your friend pulled a gun and shot the man. Before the guy died, he punched your friend out. You know yourself, sometimes a bullet don't stop a person, even after he's been shot."

How well Jake knew about shooting a man. "Thank you, sir" Jake said, as the deputy walked to his car.

Jake walked toward the courthouse, but a beat up old pickup caught his attention out of the corner of his eye. It was piled high with black plastic sacks and an old black man was bent over getting out of the seat. It was Uncle Ned.

Jake hollered "Hey you got whiskey in them bags?"

The old man looked towards him, "No sir, all I'z got is aluminum cans. Dats all," he smiled.

"Uncle Ned, it's me Jake!"

The old man put his hands on his mouth and said "Jesus, Lord Jesus you iz back! My old eyes is near bout gone, I can't see nothi'en no mo," he said smiling a big toothless smile.

"I figured you'd be in jail by now," Jake said patting the old man on his shoulder.

"I ought to be, you knows. I iz 84 years old, but have stayed out so far."

Jake shook his head in disbelief.

Uncle Ned went on, "Well the Lord iz mak'en me pay fo all dat stuff I did when I wuz young."

Jake motioned to a bench underneath a nearby shade tree, and they sat and began to talk about all the big catfish they had caught and lost. It felt good, just like old times.

"I hears your friend, dat rich boy, iz got some troubles" Uncle Ned began.

Jake looked at the old bootlegger.

"Uncle Ned, have you heard anything about it?"

"Just what da TV say, dat's all," he said dropping his head.

Jake could sense there was more, and was about to say something when there came a voice from the jail door

"Mr. Southern!" Jake held out his hand and nodded to Uncle Ned.

"I'm staying at my old boat. Come on down when you get a chance and we'll hook some of those old big cats."

Uncle Ned nodded and gave another big, toothless grin. "Sho will, sho will. Praise the Lord you is home!"

"It's good seeing you too!"

Ms T. J. Allison didn't walk, Jake thought as he watched her approach, she strutted - and what a strut!

"Could you suggest a hotel? I'm going to have to stay a few days to file some papers."

Jake replied, "don't know much about the hotels anymore, but I think the Medler's used to own The Oaks."

"Yes, that's right, they did tell me that. I'll try getting a room there."

"Okay" Jake said. "I'll be glad to take you around if you want. I'm still pretty familiar with this place, even though I've been away for some time. You could leave your car here on the court square, if you want."

"Thank you, that would be nice."

"Mr. Medler said something about you locating his friend Debbie."

Jake nodded "I'm heading over to the part of town where her family used to live to see if I can find out about her. You are more than welcome to come with me. Just get in and we'll go."

"Let me get some of my things out of the car, if you don't mind."

"No ma'amm, not at all!"

Sounded good to Jake. It would be good to have some company; especially her company.

Chapter 5

As they rode down the street, T. J. was quiet. Turning to Jake, she broke the silence: "You said you had been away for awhile. May I ask, where?"

"Yes, you may," Jake answered. All over the world really. I've just retired from the Army."

"I noticed your West Point ring", T.J. stated, looking at his ring. "What was your job in the army?"

"I was a combat commander in the Quick Response Force. We went around wherever it was hot at the time. And what about you?" he asked turning to look at her.

"There isn't much to tell. I'm a law partner with Simon, Key & Allison in Memphis. We handle mainly corporate law, but I have an extensive background in criminal law. Since the Medlers are one of our oldest and biggest accounts, I thought I would handle this one myself."

"Any gentlemen suitors waiting around?"

"No, not at the moment," she laughed thinking that he hadn't wasted much time.

A quiet settled in the car as Jake made some turns and drove slowly down an older, shady street. The area seemed unkempt and the street full of potholes. Jake thought to himself, "everything seems smaller, but everything's the same size it has always been. The difference is my world. When I was young this was my world, but now my world has grown."

"Where are we going?" T.J. asked.

"The Jenkins once lived down this street, as I remember. I'm going to see if any of Debbie's family is still around this area."

He pulled up to the curb, and parked behind an old pickup. T.J. could see some people sitting on the porch and several small children playing with a puppy in the grassless yard.

"Be right back," he told her as he got out and approached two older women and a young man.

"How are ya'll?" he asked, stopping at the bottom of the front porch steps.

"Fine", one said and the other nodded. The young man looked at Jake, not saying anything.

"I'm looking for a friend of a friend, Debra Jenkins. Ya'll know her?"

"We don't know her," the young man spoke up. "You a lawman?"

"No, a friend of mine wanted me to give her a message." Jake replied.

"Well, we can't help you buddy", the young man said frowning down at Jake.

Jake looked up and could see the shadow of a woman standing behind the screen door.

"Hello Debbie. I've been looking for you. I'm Jake, Harley's friend."

The door opened and out stepped a slender, short, brown haired, barefoot woman in a pink cotton blouse and a pair of tattered blue jean shorts.

"I remember you from school. Harley always talked about you. What can I do for you?"

"Could I talk to you over by the car?"

"Sure, why not?" she said as she came down the steps and walked over to the car.

T.J. was stepping onto the curb.

Jake introduced the two women.

"Debbie, Harley is in trouble! He said you were at Lilly's that night. Would you tell us what happened?"

"I don't know much," Debbie began. "Harley was fighting them two boys. I don't know who they was. I ain't seen nothing and don't know nothing. I was out of there in a flash when all the fightin' started. I was trying to find someone in the parking lot to help break it up."

"Harley was worried about you and said he hadn't heard from you since that night." said Jake.

"I was told that he was locked up that night but that's all I know, I just want to stay out of it!" declared Debbie with a little tremble in her voice.

"Miss Jenkins", T.J. spoke up. "Did Harley have a gun with him or did it belong to one of the other men?"

"Honey, I didn't see no gun, and I never seen Harley with one, but Harley was kinda mad cause they was messing with me. He's the one that started the ruckus by saying somthin' to em."

"Harley said he was in love with you and has been for years, since the night of our high school prom", Jake spoke up.

There was a long silence, as Debbie looked down at the ground. She finally spoke and raised her head looking toward the porch.

"That's Harley's boy standing there" she continued.

"Harley feels obligated to me, but he don't owe me nothin', and I don't owe him nothin'. I made it fine on my own for the last twenty-five years."

"Look, we messed up when we were young, and he's been trying to make up for it all these years. But love ain't in this, 'least ways not with me. I ain't ever going to be part of that big shot family of his, specially his high and mighty momma."

"Miss Jenkins, we may have to call you as a witness" T.J. said.

"Like I said, I ain't seen nothin', but you can call on me if you want."

As Debbie stepped onto the curb she turned to Jake, "Is he okay? Harley I mean."

"Yeah", Jake answered, "he's okay."

As Jake and T.J. got into the car, T.J. turned to Jake "What was that love statement all about?"

"It was just something Harley said to me at the jail, and I wanted to see her reaction. And, it seems, I got more information than I was expecting!"

"Well, it sure seems like a one way love."

Jake nodded as they pulled away from the curb.

Jake took T.J. to The Oaks and left her with a promise of dinner at 7:00. He headed back to the boat for a shower and change of clothes. His thoughts went to Debbie - what she had said and how she had said it. There seemed more to this than met the eye. Poor girl, rich boy - from two different worlds, especially in the Delta. Back in his youth it just wasn't a mix. There was race, but then there was class - the haves and the have nots. And knowing Harley's mother, if she had anything to do with it – and Jake suspected she did – that difference was made very apparent.

"If I had gone to the dance the night of the Prom would things have been different?" Jake wondered to himself. "I was right there at the door."

As his car crossed over the levy going to the boat, Jake could see some men with surveying equipment. He wondered what that was all about as he drove up to the boat. After parking the car, Jake could see a figure sitting in a chair, stooped over with a fishing pole, looking down into the water.

It was Uncle Ned!

"Hey, you old whiskey runner! You catching anything?"

Uncle Ned looked up and smiled, "Nope, but I knows he's down there. I don't think he's gonna bite cause of dat cloud of rain comin up da river."

Jake looked down river and could see the dark clouds and the rain falling below it. "Dat aughta cool things off", Uncle Ned predicted.

"Summer rain", Jake thought. "We used to pray for it when I was a kid. It would be a break from the summer heat."

"We better get inside, Uncle Ned, before we get soaked" Jake said, as the rain raced closer.

Uncle Ned put his fishing pole down and stepped inside just as the rain began to pelt the deck of the boat.

"Have a seat," Jake told his old friend.

Uncle Ned took a chair across from him. "Dis old boat sho looks good since Jessie and da Judge fixed it up", Uncle Ned looked around.

Jake smiled, "Yeah, didn't think this old boat was still floating after all these years. It was a nice surprise when the Judge brought me down to see it. You want something cool to drink? The Judge has some Cokes and beer stocked and cooled I noticed last night."

"Naw, I don't reckon", Ned replied. "You axed me 'bout what happened round here. Well, Jake I didn't zackly tell you de truth. Some folks from somewhere is buyin up every bit of 'dis riverfront and downtown as da kin get."

"Me and Jessie still fishes now and den, and he's been talkin' about folks meetin' with de Judge and stuff. But I sees peoples lookin' here and there," the old man motioned with his hand and pointed his finger to his eye.

Jake listened intently, surprised by his old friend's sharp observations and wisdom, and glad this wonderful man still had it.

"Now, 'bout yo friend. He ain't kilt nobody. I wuz at Miss Lilly's place that evening gittin' some cans. You know dem cans is sel'len for fifty cents a pound? But, it takes a bunch to make a pound."

"Anyways, I sees from the back room, and they was fighting. Da Jenkins girl she run out da do and then one of dem boys gun went off when they knocked Mr. Harley out. Da man, he throwed da gun on da flo. Den he bent over and looked at the man, den runs out the do."

"Uncle Ned," Jake said, "why didn't you stay for the police? Besides who called them?"

"Boy, you knows dem police ain't gonna listen to no old black man, specially one what's been in and out of trouble all dees years."

"Times is changed, but, I still stays away from da law."

"Naw, hit was best dat I kept my old fool mouth shut! I don't know how da law got there, I jus high tailed hit out of the back do."

Jake sat back in his chair. He was relieved.

Here was Harley's salvation. An eyewitness to what happened; this would wrap the case up for T.J and free Harley.

Jake looked at his watch; T.J. and dinner were waiting.

"Uncle Ned, I want you to talk to somebody tomorrow morning about this. Where are you staying these days?"

Ned looked alarmed, "You ain't bring'in da law is you?"

"No. No. It's Harley's lawyer. She'll want to hear what you told me, that's all."

"I don't know", the old man said shaking his head.

"Uncle Ned," Jake spoke up, "all those years when I was selling your whiskey, did I ever once mention your name? Did I always keep your money straight? Haven't we always trusted one another? I need you to help my friend. Please, for me?"

Ned looked at Jake, "Boy, you's a salesman, dat you is. All right, bring dat big shot lawyer on by to talk. I stays in a back room of dat old fish market down on Welson street. I'll be there in da morning."

"Thanks Uncle Ned. Do you need anything?"

"Naw boy, I'z got twenty dollars, a full bottle of snuff, and fo dollar worf of gas in dat old pickup. What else do an old man need? Septin, maybe to talk sometimes. Dats tha onlyest thing about getting' old is, you is got a lot to say, but nobody wants to hear it!"

Chapter 6

Jake noticed the summer shower was moving on to the north as the roll and grumble of the thunder became more distant. He walked to the door and patted his old friend on the back saying goodbye and that he would see him in the morning.

Uncle Ned walked down the wet marina as Jake remembered all the days they had spent together in his youth - good days!

The heat was coming back as the summer shower passed, leaving a steamy light fog over the river. He'd better hurry to get ready for his dinner date.

Jake walked up to the front desk and could see the clock on the wall showing 7:30. He was running late. He shook his head and thought to himself that this wasn't like him at all. He never ran late.

He approached the clerk, asking for Ms. Allison's room. The clerk replied that she was not in her room. She had left a message for him to meet her in the dining room.

Walking into the dining room, he could see T.J. sitting at a table with Mr. Medler, Miss Anna and Harley. Harley saw Jake and stood up and shook Jake's hand.

"How did you get out?" Jake asked.

"My lawyer convinced the judge to set bail and dad posted it." Harley answered. "Have you found Debbie?"

"Yeah, she was at her mother's old house."

"Is she okay?"

"Yes, best as I could tell, Harley."

"Harley," Miss Anna spoke up. Jake could tell by the look on her face and the firmness in her voice that she wanted to change the conversation.

Jake shook Mr. Medler's hand as everyone settled in their seats for dinner. Jake looked over at T.J. and nodded.

T.J. pointed to her watch and smiled.

Jake smiled and said, "Sorry! I've got some good news," he spoke up as he placed his napkin in his lap.

"I've found someone who saw what happened in that bar and he is willing to talk to you in the morning."

"Who?" Harley asked leaning forward.

"Uncle Ned," Jake replied.

Mr. Medler spoke up, "That old black man that gathers cans around town? And wasn't he into some bootlegger back when the state was dry?"

"Yes sir, the same one. He's the man that is going to keep your son out of jail."

"And keep your son from going to trial," T. J. spoke up. "How did you find this out Jake? Is that the old man you were talking to outside the jail?"

"Yes, he's an old friend of mine,"

"We had a long chat when he came to my boat today. That's why I was running late."

"That's great news," Harley said smiling.

Miss Anna spoke up, "I don't see how an old ex-whiskey runner and bum, who collects cans, is going to be believed!"

"I believe him," Jake said looking at her. "He's my friend and has been for many years. He's always been honest. And he is no bum."

As if to break the chill and tension in the air T.J. spoke up, "Ms. Medler, if we have an eyewitness to what happened that night, we have a good chance of clearing Harley, no matter who the witness is. It's up to the state to prove his unreliability."

"What does he want for this?" Miss Anna asked looking with disdain at Jake.

"Nothing - he wants nothing ma'am."

"This is fantastic," Mr. Medler spoke up.

"Jake, thank you for finding out about this, son. We weren't sure what we were going to do. Let's have a bite to eat," he said as the waitress walked over to the table.

"A double bourbon for me. Anyone else? Jake, how about you?"

"No thanks, Mr. Medler, I don't drink," Jake answered. T.J. glanced at him over her menu.

After dinner and light, polite conversation, Harley looked at his watch and stood up. "If you' all will pardon me, I've got to run."

Miss Anna spoke up, "Harley, you need to get some rest from your ordeal. Honey, are you going home?"

"No mother, I'll be home later. I've got something to do."

"Honey, I hope it's not going to see that girl. You should stay away from her for awhile."

Harley cut her short, "Mother, we have had this conversation many times before and it's not going to change my view."

Looking at Jake, he said, "I'll catch you later friend" and smiled, looking at T.J.

"Thanks for everything, T. J., I'll be talking to you tomorrow."

After Harley left, Miss Anna stood and walked out of the room, Mr. Medler followed her, looking back to say his good-byes to everyone.

"Thanks for the good news. We enjoyed the dinner," and they were gone.

Jake and T.J. were alone at the table and Jake ordered coffee.

"Jake, there seems to be a little bit of a tiff over Harley's social life."

"Guess Harley has been through that all of his life," Jake explained. "First being my friend, and now apparently with this Debbie thing. Must be the price you pay for being a Medler and Miss Anna's son," he smiled.

Changing the subject, Jake chuckled, "I guess this place is boring after the big city life. Not to much to do around here, is there?"

"Oh, I don't know. If I were home I would be looking over briefs or washing clothes," T.J. answered.

Jake smiled, "For some reason I can't picture you operating a washing machine."

"Well," she said, "somebody has to do the laundry. And I don't have maid service."

"What about you" she asked? "It's got to be a slower pace than you are used to."

"Yeah, I guess. Over the last few years it's been Saudi Arabia this week then on to the Pentagon; a midnight call and trouble in Bosnia, and the next thing is coffee on a C140 in the wee hours of the morning flying across the Atlantic. This is a tad bit slower, but I guess it's time for me to slow down."

They talked on about her life as a lawyer, her failed marriages, his life in the military, places he had been and seen.

Jake thought, as he listened to T.J. "I've never slowed down enough to reflect on where I've been or what I've done, much less talk about it. This feels good. This is what retirement is all about." And he settled into his chair.

The waitress walked up to the table and asked if there was anything else she could get them. Jake and T.J. looked around and noticed they were the only two remaining and the restaurant was about to close for the evening. Jake glanced at his watch and apologized to the waitress for staying so late. They got up and walked out into the evening. The stars were so bright Neither could remember when they had enjoyed an evening so much in a long time.

"Jake," T.J. spoke up, "Could I get you to drive me to my car? I'm going to need it tomorrow."

"Sure, no problem."

As they drove along, Jake could see the moon shining through the trees along the street.

"You mind going somewhere? It won't take long, or are you too tired?" Jake asked.

"No, as a matter a fact, I'm feeling great!" she replied "Where are we going?"

"Out to a point at a bend in the river. The Corps of Engineers built a tower there years ago. I want to see if it's still there."

"Sounds great!"

They pulled off the main road onto a country lane surrounded by moonlit trees and drove over the levee, and out into an opening. There at the end of the road was a square structure with stairs leading to the top. They both got out of the car and walked up the path and proceeded up the stairway to the top of the tower. From the height at the top of the tower, one could see the moonlight shining onto the river, causing it to shimmer as it wound and bent its way far down to the sea. They both stood perfectly still as the night surrounded them.

Jake could smell the honeysuckle and hear the frogs singing in unison with the chirping choir of a million crickets. He thought to himself, "This hasn't changed." It was exactly the same look, the same sounds and smells he had always remembered.

T.J. said softly, "This is nice."

"Yeah, and the breeze from the river keeps the mosquitoes away," added Jake.

"You must have spent a lot of time along this river as a boy."

"Pretty much, when I wasn't making a living and going to school. But it's been a big part of my life as a man too.

I've thought about this spot in a lot of day dreams in a lot of lousy places."

"Never about the pretty girl you left behind?" T. J. asked. "No old loves?"

"No, I didn't leave anyone special behind. There have been people in my life that I guess I loved, but not like you're talking about."

"Any more special places like this one?" T.J. asked looking out at the river.

"Maybe one. Maybe one very special place.

Jake looked at his watch, he said, "It's getting late, or I should say early in the morning. I'd better get you back."

When they began to walk towards the stairs, T.J. turned and looked into his khaki colored eyes and said, "Thank you for sharing this with me, Jake." She kissed his cheek.

He saw T.J. to the door of her room and then drove to the marina and walked to the boat. When he stepped inside, he saw Harley leaning back in the rocking chair asleep. "Hey boy," Jake shook him, "get up and go to bed."

Harley jumped with a startled look that soon settled into a grin. "You been with that looker lawyer of mine buddy? Never seen you with a woman before. You were always too busy!"

Jake settled into a comfortable armchair. "You haven't been around me for a long time hoss."

Harley said, "Remember that time we caught that old cotton picker bus and picked cotton all day long? Our hands were all scratched up from reaching for those cotton bolls, and my shoulder still aches from pulling that nine-foot cotton sack and it cutting into my shoulder. And remember how good and cold that water tasted out of the big glass jug wrapped with wet burlap? And that little black girl that kept giving you the eye?"

"The things you got me into, Harley!" Jake remembered, "But she was kinda cute."

Harley leaned forward, "I think a lot about those days, Jake. You were the closest thing to a brother I ever had. And in a way, I was envious of you for having the ability to lead a real life."

Leaning back, he said, "Remember that evening we were riding in the old Lincoln convertible, racing down the dirt roads and came across old man Fowler's watermelon patch? I stopped the car and the dust rolled over the whole car, nearly choked us to death. We both jumped out and went to grabbing watermelons and throwing them into the back seat as fast as we could. We drove to the Indian mounds, got up on the top of that big mound and ate the hearts out of those melons. I can still see that juice all over our shirts and faces. Then we laid back and watched the stars. Man, those were good watermelons!"

They both laughed and remembered.

"Harley, what is this thing about you and Debbie? She says her son is yours."

Harley looked down. "She has never said that to me!"

"It started that night at our high school prom. One thing led to another. We kept seeing each other off and on throughout the years."

"When I found out she was pregnant, I went to my folks and told them. Mom threw a fit and said a lot of stupid things. Dad said if I married her I was out on my own. You know the story. Looking down he said; "I chose first to be Harley Medler, III, instead of responsibility. Ever since college I've tried to make it up to Debbie and the boy, but it hasn't done any good. She said I let my family make my life. But she doesn't understand the responsibilities I have to my family and to this community and pretty soon to this whole part of our state."

"What about your son, Harley?" Jake asked quietly. "You did what you always used to complain that your dad was doing, putting your business and family's name before your son!"

Harley looked down but didn't respond.

"Hey," Jake said changing the subject, "I've got an early morning appointment to show that good-looking lawyer of yours where Uncle Ned, your key witness, lives. She says she wants to talk to him."

"Grab a bed and you can buy us all breakfast with all that money you've got!"

Jake got up and slapped his friend's shoulder, "Let's hit the sack. You take the bunk in there!"

Early the next morning Jake and Harley drove to The Oaks Hotel. They found T.J. in the restaurant having breakfast. She was looking over some papers. "Hi guys. Sleep well?"

"Fine, thank you, what about you?" Jake spoke up.

"You want to ride with us to Uncle Ned's or follow after we eat a bite?"

"I'll ride with you guys if it's okay."

"Sure thing. I suppose you two had a lot to catch up on?"

"You don't get much out of this guy! He's still the shy, quiet type," Harley said, looking at Jake.

They finished their breakfast, then got into the car and began their drive. Jake turned onto Nelson Street that once led to the old portion of what was known as the black part of town. He could see the fish market. Parked beside the market was an ambulance, two police cars and a dozen or so people. He pulled his car up behind the ambulance and they all got out.

"What's going on?" Jake asked as he walked up to one of the policemen.

"An old guy must have had a heart attack in his sleep, according to the medic. One of the young boys that bring him coffee in the morning found him. Said he couldn't wake the old man up so he called us and we called an ambulance," the policeman informed Jake. "The medic said he's been dead about four hours."

T.J. looked at Harley. "Don't worry. I've got some other things up my sleeve."

Jake walked over to the stretcher and uncovered his friend's face. Looking at him, he leaned over and said goodbye to Uncle Ned.

"I know you're where all the catfish are fat now," then covered his old friend again.

Jake could feel T.J.'s hand on his arm.

As they got back into the car and began driving away, Harley turned to T.J. "What now? That was my witness. How big of a mess am I in now?"

"Harley, did you get checked for gun powder on your hands when you were taken to jail?" she asked.

"No, I don't think I was."

"I'm going to see what Mr. Twill, the prosecutor, has got and by that I'll determine what they don't have," T.J. said.

Jake pulled his car up to the curb at the courthouse and everyone began to get out. A large dark sedan pulled into the space behind them. On the sides of the sedan were signs reading "Vote - B. Thomas Twill - Attorney General".

Jake looked at the slender figure of a man getting out of the car. He could still remember Twill from his childhood. He was much older now with dark, dyed, hair that had been combed over to conceal his balding head. He wore wire-rimmed glasses and had a weasel face. Jake remembered that he didn't like him as a kid, and he still felt the same way.

"Hello, Mr. Twill. Jake Southern," Jake said offering his hand. "This is Mr. Medler's attorney, T.J. Allison."

"How do you do?" Twill said in his irritating, shrill voice.

"What can I do for you?"

T.J. spoke up, " Mr. Twill, I'd like information on what you have on my client."

"In due time, young lady. In due time," he smiled.

"Mr. Twill," T.J. went on, "with all due respect, I need what you have to prepare a defense, as soon as possible, please."

"Very well, I'll have my secretary get you a copy. Where should I send it? You aren't from here, are you?" he asked looking down his nose.

"No, I'm from Memphis," T.J. answered. "But I'm staying at The Oaks."

Of course you are, of course," Twill said with a jerk of his body, quickly turning and walking away toward the court, as if dismissing them from his presence.

Harley spoke up, "What a jerk!"

Jake smiled and said, "He was always a jerk as best as I remember. But that old jerk can send you to jail."

"Well, look." Harley said. "I've got to go over to the bank."

T.J. took leave to go and talk further with Twill saying she was going to try and rush him along with the information. Both men watched as she walked away. Harley said, what Jake was thinking, "Now that's a walk!"

"I'll catch up with you later," Harley said as he crossed the street to the bank. Jake looked at his watch. It was 10:00 am. The Judge should be in. He walked toward the courthouse.

Jake was about to introduce himself to the Judge's secretary, when, from the Judge's office, came his voice.

"Come on in son. Christy, this is Jake Southern."

Jake nodded to her and smiled as she went back to her work.

The Judge was putting on his robe when Jake walked through the open door of his office.

"Have a seat son. What's been going on? We've been looking for you to come up to the house. Della is mad that you didn't eat with us last night."

"Sir, do you remember Uncle Ned?"

"Yes, we are long and old acquaintances. Why?"

"He died last night."

"My goodness, I'm so sorry to hear that. He was quite the character, and he was on up in years. What happened?"

"The Medic said it was his heart", Jake said with a sad tone to his voice.

"I'm sorry to hear that. I remember you and he were friends and he was a friend of Jessie's too."

"Thank you, sir. I'm glad I got to visit with him one last time. I have some good memories of our times together. He saw what happened at Lilly's and was Harley's only eye witness."

"Son, I can't discuss anything about Harley's trial with you. But I am sorry about his death," the Judge sympathized.

The Judge sat down behind his desk while buttoning his robe.

"Sir," Jake spoke up, "what's happening to this part of the country? I see businesses closed and the town seems to be getting run down. When I was going over the levy, I saw a survey crew working."

"You've been gone a long time," the Judge began. "We are changing around here. We used to depend on farming and the business that supported farming. Even though there is still lots of farming going on, it doesn't require as much manpower anymore."

The Judge settled into his chair, "Most of the textile plants have moved out of the states to Mexico or who knows where. We're trying to readjust ourselves. There are some things in the works that your friend Harley's family are into that we all hope will revitalize this town and bring some jobs back." The Judge went on, "you know gambling was voted in along the river, and that river port is a prime location. To answer your question about the surveyors, I'm not really sure."

Jake was quiet for a moment, "Sir," he spoke up. "If most of the town's industry is gone, where are the people around here going to get money to gamble and sustain a casino?"

"That's true, but what I hear is that people from all over would be coming. Sort of like that old saying, 'Build it and they will come'."

I didn't know about the Medler's getting into gambling," Jake said. "Harley didn't mention business to me."

"Well," the Judge spoke up, "they may not be, if he's convicted of shooting that boy. He's a full partner in the Medler business, and if convicted their company will not get a gaming license."

"What do you mean, asked Jake?"

"If a company applies for a gaming license and anyone who is head of that firm has any kind of criminal record or conviction, they are eliminated. The reason being, the government is trying to keep any criminal element from coming in and getting a foot-hold," the Judge explained.

"Well," said the Judge after a pause, "how'd you like that boat of yours?"

"Great! You and Jessie have done a wonderful job, and I appreciate the work you put in her. But sir, I walked away from her a long time ago and by all rights she is yours."

"Aw bull, son! What do I need that old boat for? Besides you need a place to stay and it's your home. I won't hear anything about that old rust bucket being mine." As he smiled and stood up, he added, "now, you come on up to the house for supper when you get through running around today or Della is going to hunt you down and drag you home."

"Yes sir, I'll be there."

"Sir, do you mind if I bring Harley's attorney?"

The Judge smiled. "I heard she is a looker. And smart too, from what I gather from my old lawyer friends up north."

Jake knew the Judge meant anything north of the county line was "up north". A smile came to his face as he thought about this.

"Yes sir, she is, and we'll be there at, say around 7:00?"

"Fine, fine," the Judge said. "I'll call Della and let her know. In the meantime, I have got to get into court," he said as he opened the wood paneled door and Jake heard "all rise" as the door closed.

Jake walked out of the courthouse and took a seat on a bench under one of the large oak trees on the court square.

He looked around at all the old, familiar buildings. There was the movie theater, drug store, five and dime, and the bank. But for some reason these places didn't have the life, the shine that he remembered from his boyhood.

"What are you thinking about?" T.J. said as she walked up and sat down beside him.

"I was thinking how much smaller the world gets as we get older."

"What did you find out?"

"The hearing is set for tomorrow and I've got to get to work," she said.

"What are you going to do?" Jake asked.

"First, take this stuff (holding up a folder of papers) and read it. Then plan my strategy."

"T.J.," do you know anything about the Medler family getting a gaming license from the state gaming commission?"

"Well, yes," she answered, "our firm took care of the legal work and applied for them. Not a lot of people know about it around here. How did you hear?"

"Well," Jake continued, "I heard a little bird talking about it. Anyway, could someone have set Harley up is the question I'm asking? Could all this be about discrediting the Medler Corporation and spoiling their chances of getting that license?"

"I knew Harley growing up, and I'm positive he's not capable of what he is charged with."

"Jake, I'll let you in on something," T.J. continued. "We have people checking into that very idea as we speak. With the money that we're talking about in potential profits, it's very likely that there could be some type of conspiracy. What I do know is the identity of the man Harley allegedly shot. It has come from a FBI industrial espionage list. And he was an ex-convict from California. Now why would an ex-con who deals in industrial espionage be in a beer joint way down in the Mississippi Delta?"

Jake thought, "This gal is on the ball. No doubt she knows how to earn her money."

"You leave me speechless T.J., and for that information you just entrusted me with, I'm taking you to supper at the home of the great Judge Nathan Buford Cole. Loosen your corset, cause he's got, as I remember, the greatest cook in these parts, or for that matter, anywhere!"

Chapter 7

ॐ

Jake could see movement from the kitchen, as he knocked on the screen door. "Ya'll come on in," he heard Della say as he opened the door for T.J.

"Da Judge, he upstairs so ya'll come on in da kitchen so as I can look at you, while I iz cookin!"

"How do you do?" Della said looking at T.J. "You da lawyer for dat Harley boy? Da Judge say Jake was bringin' you."

"Yes Della," Jake spoke up. This is T.J. Allison from Memphis, and I haven't told her how mean you are yet, so be sweet!"

"Hush boy! You knows I iz sweet as mo-lasses," she said smiling.

"Since dat child's po momma died, I iz been watchen him, cause I told her I would, God rest her soul. She was sho a good woman! I knowed her when dis boy was a baby. She hep me with dem girl's what couldn't pay no doctor to bring da babies into this world. She went to school for real nursen, and she knowed lots bout dat."

"What's all this racket?" Judge Cole said smiling as he walked into the kitchen.

"Judge, this is T.J. Allison."

"We spoke on the phone, sir," T.J. said, reaching to shake his hand. "Thank you for having Jake show me around."

"I don't think Jake has minded at all Miss Allison! I see you've met Della."

"Now, you all get out a my kitchen so's I ken get dis food on da table. Sept you Jake, I need you to stay. I needs to talk to you," Della commanded.

T.J. and the Judge left the kitchen to go into the parlor. As soon as they were gone and Della felt they couldn't hear what she said, she began. "I ain't spose to say dis, but you is got to know," Della said in a whisper. "Da Judge ain't gonna be with us much mo."

"What do you mean Della?"

"He gonna die is what I'm a sayen child. I heard da doctor tell him three weeks ago. Lord boy, he die'n! Dat's why I sent for you, cause you is closest to kin he is got, septin' me and Jessie. Dis here stuff bout yo friend come afterwards."

Jake sat down in a chair by the table, his legs suddenly weak.

"How long has he got?" he asked looking at her as she wiped tears from her eyes with her crisp, white apron.

"Dat's what da Judge ax da doctor, honey. He say some folks goes slow and other folks goes fast. Den he say maybe six months, maybe mo. Child, we is been wit dat man most of us's life, sept when he was in da war. Dats been better'en fifty years. He always a tell'en me and Jessie we is took care of if'en sump'en was ta happen to him, but we ain't studying dat. Dat man is like my own. I jus was, jus want'en you to know. You is as close to a child to him as anyone is and I knows how dat man feels bout you."

Again she wiped tears away as they streamed down her round, sweet, brown face.

"Thank you for telling me, Della. Is there anything I can do?"

"Jus spend some time wit him. Dat's all I can think of."

Rising from his chair, Jake hugged Della.

Jake stepped into the parlor where T.J. and the Judge were sitting.

"The Judge was telling me some interesting things about you. He said you've been on your own since you were fourteen years old," T.J. said seeing Jake enter the room. "I was thinking that's a very young age for anyone to be by themselves."

"He wasn't exactly alone, T.J." the Judge replied. This boy was full grown at fourteen. You couldn't find anyone any better to work, and I might add, keep up his school work."

"I figured he was pretty smart to get into West Point," T.J. said.

"Not all that smart," Jake spoke up. "The Judge had something to do with that, not my smarts."

The judge interjected, "Your grades were right at the top of your class."

"Dinners on da table!" came Della's voice from the dinning room. "Ya'll come on in fo it gets cold."

The dinner was as wonderful as Jake had remembered Della's cooking from his youth. She had made all his favorites: fried chicken, creamed potatoes and gravy, her famous homemade yeast rolls, and, fresh from her garden in back of the house came summer tomatoes, corn, and fried okra. And for dessert, fresh peach cobbler served with home-made vanilla ice ream, which Jessie had hand cranked that afternoon. Oh, he was in heaven!

Getting up from the table T.J. began stacking the dirty plates.

Della said, "Honey, you ain't spose to do that."

"No, I insist Della. After a meal like that, I need to work some of it off. That was one of the best meals I have had in a long while," T.J. said smiling.

"Well son," the Judge said looking at Jake. "I'm not that full, are you?" they both laughed. "Let's go out and sit on the porch for awhile."

Seated on the front porch in the big rockers, one could hear the soft rolling noise of the locus, crickets, and frogs as they sang their night songs. It was real peace on earth, sitting, rocking slowly, with your stomach satisfied from a delicious meal, and relaxing, finally slowing down.

"Sir," Jake spoke first. "Della told me about the doctor coming over and what he said."

"That woman," the Judge said shaking his head.

"What's wrong? Is there something that can be done?"

"No, not a thing."

After a pause, the Judge began, "Doc says it's something that eats away at the heart muscle. The back part of my heart muscle has died; I forget what he called it exactly. I'm okay with it. I mean there is no pain or bad stuff. I've pretty well got everything in order, except maybe talking to you," he said with a soft smile.

"You didn't know this, but I was at your graduation at West Point. You being the number one graduate, you were a very busy young man that day. Besides, I didn't want to be in your way."

"No, I didn't known sir. As I recall there were hundreds of people there. If I had known . . ."

"No", the Judge cut him off as he reached over to touch Jake's arm. "It was me son, I wanted it that way. I wanted you to make it through life in your own way after graduation day. Even after your folks died, I could have made you move in with us, but I thought that it was time to let you start learning about life on your own. And I might add, you did pretty well at it. Even selling Uncle Ned's whiskey," he said with a laugh.

"How did you find out about that?" Jake smiled.

"There isn't much that goes on in this county that I didn't know about back then," the Judge stated.

"Sir, how do you feel about dying?" Jake asked.

"I'm not crazy about the idea of course, but I've had a full and rewarding life. I've fought a war, loved some find women, drank some good bourbon with some great friends. I think I've done some worthwhile things while I've been on this earth, and I'm at peace with God. I believe if a man can say all that, and if it's true, he can go in peace, don't you think?"

"Yes sir," Jake said with a smile. "I agree."

They sat and rocked in silence for a long while, each in their own thoughts.

Some time later T.J. and Della came outside and sat on the old porch swing. Jessie came around the side of the house, sat on the steps, and leaned back against the banister. They talked about how pleasant it was after a hot summer day, but mainly they sat and listened to the sounds of the night and smelled the honeysuckle. Off in the distance they could hear the cooing of the doves settling in for the evening.

Chapter 8

Jake was awake early the next morning. With a hot cup of coffee in his hand, he walked out onto the deck and took a seat, and watched the morning steam rise from the river. His thoughts went back to the disheartening news about the Judge. There was so much more he wanted to say to him.

He wanted to tell him of the respect he held for him; how much it had meant to have him listen to all his petty boyhood problems; how much it meant, knowing the Judge was always there, and yes, to say "Sir, I love you! I love you for stepping in when both parents died, being a father, a friend, and my rock - always firm and steady!"

Why couldn't he say these things, instead of saying something stupid like, "How do you feel about dying?"

In every combat engagement in his military career he had thought about dying. He had made peace with God, accepted his fate, and hoped if death came, it would be quick. He thought about all these years - the time away, the missed opportunities, sending post cards rather than letters, seeing the world instead of coming to visit.

"Now at least I'm here at the end of his journey."

Then his thoughts suddenly shifted, "Jake Southern, you old dog," he thought to himself. "You sat there in the car as T.J. kissed you goodnight, let her slip out of the car, walked her to her room, and you didn't try anything, not one smooth move! Old boy, you must be getting old! Maybe there's just too much going on."

Glancing at the rising sun, then at his watch, he took another sip of coffee.

"What about Harley's situation? I've got to get one thing settled at a time," he realized.

Jake recalled meeting Harley for the first time, sometime around the fourth grade. The three Blain brothers had Harley cornered on the schoolyard. The biggest of the Blain boys, Rudy, had pushed Harley down and the other two were urging their big brother on.

Jake shook his head and laughed thinking back. He had walked up to Rudy and hit him right straight in the nose. Rudy looked like a raccoon with those two blackened eyes and that swollen nose for two weeks. As Rudy lay on the ground holding his nose, the younger Blain boy asked Jake, "Why did you do that?"

Jake had replied, "Cause Harley's my friend."

It's been a long time since the fourth grade.

He could still recall the 'talking to' when he got home that evening from his mom.

He smiled, finished his morning coffee, and went in to get ready to go downtown for the day.

"I've got to get my mind on Harley's problem and get things together" he reasoned to himself.

"Nobody is above the law in this state," Twill said into a microphone held in front of him by a news reporter. "All of Mr. Medler's money won't help him out of this. I will prove Mr. Medler killed in cold blood while in a drunken rage."

"Where you from?" Jake asked a technician holding some wires in his hand.

"Jackson," the man replied. "We got a scoop that there was a big hearing today. Some rich boy is up for murder. This guy talking, I'm told, is running for some state office, I think. He's probably the one that called us about the story," the man said with a knowing smile.

"Thanks," Jake nodded to the technician as he walked into the courthouse and made his way upstairs to the courtroom. In the courtroom, he walked up to T.J. who was standing reading some papers. Harley was seated at the table. T.J. looked up from the papers and smiled, then went back to reading. Jake put his hand on Harley's shoulder.

"How are you partner?"

Jake could tell by the dark circles under his eyes that he hadn't slept well the night before.

"So far I'm okay, Jake. I'm glad you are here!"

Jake walked back to the benches, pausing to speak to Mr. Medler and Miss Anna before being seated.

"All rise," said the bailiff. Everyone stood as Judge Cole entered the room and took his seat.

"Wonder if he still packs that cannon," Jake thought.

As the clerk read the charges, a middle-aged man in a sports jacket and open collar shirt walked by Jake and up to T.J. He leaned over whispering to her. T.J. sat erect and Jake could tell she was interested by this man's news.

"Your honor," T.J. said standing up.

"Yes, Miss Allison," the Judge replied.

"I've just been given some information that will have a great bearing on this case. If I can have a couple of hours recess to check out this information it would have a tremendous bearing on my client's behalf."

"Objection," Twill shouted. We have all the evidence there is your honor."

The Judge asked the two attorneys to approach the bench.

"Mr. Twill," the Judge spoke. "Look at it from this perspective. You can take this time to talk to the news media."

"I'm going to grant you a couple of hours Miss Allison. A recess of this hearing is granted for two hours," the Judge said hammering down his gavel and turning to disappear into his chamber's door.

Jake walked up to the table where the man with the message was again talking to T.J.

She stopped and introduced Jake.

"This is Mr. Newborn. He works for my firm as a private investigator. He has some news for us."

Mr. Newborn began, "The dead man and his brother-in-law work for an Asian investment company that also has applied for a gaming license. The gun found at the scene was registered to the dead man's sister. I spoke to her on the phone and she said her husband called last night from a motel thirty miles from here. The sheriff had a deputy go pick him up, and after awhile he confessed that he and the dead man had wanted to set Harley up. They were offered ten thousand dollars to get some dirt on the Medlers, and Harley was their easiest target. They knew he came to the bar sometimes to see a lady, and they planned to get him into a fight. One would pull the gun and would wound the other, blame Harley, get the Medler's into court and make big headlines. They would get ten thousand. But it seems they didn't plan on the one getting shot to have a main artery severed in his leg and bleed to death."

T.J. spoke up, "Did the sheriff record his confession?"

"Yes ma'am, the Judge should be reviewing it now."

"The people he was working for - who are they?" Jake asked.

He claims he doesn't know. Said some Asian guy talked to them, gave them one thousand a piece, and told them when he read about some scandal in the newspaper involving the Medlers, he would contact them and pay them the rest," Mr. Newborn continued.

That's the way these things work. Someone is always in the shadows and the dummies out front."

Jake turned to Harley and smiled. "Well buddy, it seems you skimmed by on this one!"

Harley could only shake his head. As his mother and father walked up behind T. J., she turned to give them the news.

Miss Anna was excited and decided to throw a party for the occasion. "All of you please come to the house this evening and we'll celebrate."

She looked directly at Jake as she spoke, "Jake, please come." Jake wondered to himself if he had finally made himself worthy in Ms. Medler's eyes? Then he asked himself the question, "did he really care?" "No."

Chapter 9

Jake grabbed one side of the wooden box as Jessie and two other men held the other corners and walked to the open grave. Della, the preacher and a young boy stood to one side of the grave.

Each man, taking the ends of the rope, lowered the box into the ground. Each man stepped back, and the preacher began to speak.

"Lord, accept this man into yo bosom. You knows him like you knows us all!" Jake's mind wandered back to his long conversations with Uncle Ned, as they sat on the banks of the river.

One day Jake had picked up a smooth, round rock and was turning it over and over in his hands, looking at it. He had asked Uncle Ned, "How did this rock get so smooth?

He would never forget Uncle Ned's answer.

"Life boy. All dat rock's life it's been rolled around and banged on till it come out round and smooth. Dat's da way life is. In da end we hopes we gonna be just as smooth as dat rock. But first we is got to go through the bangin' of life."

"Amen," said the preacher as he finished his prayer.

After the brief service, Della introduced the young boy to Jake as Bobby.

"Yea," the young man spoke up. "I heard Uncle Ned talk about you being some General dude in the Army."

Jake smiled and corrected, "Colonel dude. I'm pleased to meet you," he said reaching to shake his hand. "Are you a relative of Uncle Ned's?"

"Naw, we were in business together. He's helped me out since my folk's died in a car wreck and all. That old man, he made me stay in school."

Jake smiled as he shook the young man's hand. "Uncle Ned was still helping strays," he thought.

It was getting late in the evening when he went to meet T.J. at her hotel. They began the drive to the Medler's home. The drive was rather quiet as Jake reflected back on the funeral earlier in the day.

"Sorry I couldn't stay around this afternoon for court," Jake began, "but it sounded as if you had things pretty well wrapped up. How did everything go?"

"Mr. Twill was upset," T.J. laughed. The Judge dismissed the charges against Harley after he heard the man's statement. I missed seeing you there. Where were you?"

"Saying goodbye to an old friend," Jake answered.

"T.J. I want to ask you something."

"Yes?"

"I know you'll be wanting to get back to Memphis pretty soon, and well, I know you don't know much about me, but I've got this trip planned to Hawaii, and I was wondering if your would be interested in going?"

She looked at him and smiled. "You know what, Mr. Southern, I think I would enjoy that! But first I have to clear up some work."

"Well, I'll be tying up some things around here for awhile too, but I'll give you a call about the details later if it's okay with you."

"Sounds wonderful, and it sounds as if we have a plan!"

"Yes we do!" he said as he smiled at her.

They had arrived at the Medler's. Walking up to the door of the grand Medler home, Jake couldn't help but notice all the cars parked along the large circle drive. "Looks like quite a crowd," he said looking at T.J.

They walked thru the opened door into the foyer, with its chandelier gleaming from the high ceiling. "From the minute you walk in, it still makes you feel very small," Jake thought.

Miss Anna greeted them, "Good of you to come." She shook T.J.'s hand and looked towards Jake and nodded.

"It's good to see you too Jake. Come on into the recreation room where everyone is."

"Where is Harley?" Jake asked.

He looked around the room, but didn't see his friend.

"He left a short while ago, said he had to pick up something, and he would be back," Miss Anna answered.

Mr. Medler walked up smiling, "fine job, young lady, fine job," and hugged T.J.

"We are glad you both are here. Let me introduce you to some of our friends."

As they mixed and mingled with the dozen or so people in the room, Jake kept looking toward the door. Then he saw Harley walking in with Debbie.

"Hey everybody!" he exclaimed, "Glad you are all here. Sorry I'm a bit late, but I had to pick up my date."

Miss Anna's face began to flush and she looked as if she was about to explode, but she walked over and spoke to Debbie. "Nice to see you again," she managed to say with a weak smile.

Harley spoke up. "For those of you who don't know, this lady is Debbie. We have a son together!"

The room was totally quiet for a moment.

"Jake," Harley said as he walked over, bear-hugged him and whispered, "keep an eye on mom. She's probably going to pass out any minute!"

Backing off, Harley winked.

"How did this come about?" Jake asked.

"I'll tell you about it later. He took Debbie by the arm and started introducing her around the room.

Jake turned and was looking out the french doors onto an open patio. He could see old Mr. Medler talking to an Asian man. They stood and talked briefly, then shook hands.

The Asian man walked away.

Noticing Jake, Mr. Medler Sr. walked to the door where he stood.

"Good to see you Jake. Business doesn't stop even when you get old," he said nodding toward the patio.

"Yes sir, so it seems," Jake replied.

As they turned around facing the room, old Mr. Medler said, "I see Harley's back."

"Yes sir. He's brought a guest."

"Well, good for him!" said the old man.

"Sir," Jake spoke. "I'm glad it turned out okay for Harley."

Mr. Medler looked at Jake. "Son, there was no doubt it was going to turn out okay for him."

"I'm sorry sir. I don't understand what you mean. It didn't look good for Harley for a while."

Old Mr. Medler smiled. "Son, I wouldn't let that boy go to jail if it took every cent we have. A lot of things have changed in this part of the world, but money still moves mountains."

"Are you saying Harley was bought out of this sir?"

"No, not exactly, but I did find out who was involved in this. I am just saying if I had to, I would have paid dearly. I'm also not implying your friend Judge Cole could be bought. All these years of knowing him, there hasn't been any time that I know of that anyone has ever gotten to him. He's unreachable! And he was the only hurdle we were dreading. And I'm glad we didn't have to go there.

"But," the old man continued, "that's the reason he's still just a local county judge. He's got too much pride and pigheaded principles to move up in the world. I've told him that for years."

Jake spoke up, "Maybe he's satisfied just where he is?"

"Well, maybe! Enough politics. Let's just enjoy the get-together, shall we?"

Harley and Debbie walked over to Jake and Mr. Medler. Harley introduced Debbie to his grandfather.

"So nice to meet you in person," Mr. Medler said. "You're the young lady that has been the talk of this family for a long while, and, I might add, such an attractive one! It's a pleasure to finally meet you in person."

"Sir," Debbie smiled. "Thank you. I've seen you around town all of my life, but never had a chance to meet you."

Harley spoke up, "Now that you've met Granddad, I know for sure you are going to be seeing a lot more of him if he has anything to say about it."

"Well," old Mr. Medler spoke up. "You two boys catch up on old times, and I'm taking Debbie over for some refreshments."

As Harley walked away looking back at Mr. Medler holding Debbie's arm, he turned to Jake. "I got to thinking the other night on that old boat of yours about what you said. You said I was turning out like my dad. Man, did you hit the nail on the head. When I found out I was out of that shooting business, I headed straight for Debbie's and talked to her and the boy. I told Debbie I wanted to start fresh, putting my family's business out of my personal life. Even though I am a Medler, my life is my own, and I'm going to start living it that way. She was quiet for awhile and then she said to me, "Harley, my name is Debbie. Would you like to go out some time?"

Jake put his hand on Harley's shoulder and smiled. "Way to go Harley! It's about time."

"Debbie said on the way over here that our son wants to go to college but he could never afford it. She is set against me giving him the money. However I'm going to put in for a couple of scholarships that my family supports."

"Kinda of a back-door approach," Jake said, "but it sounds as if you're getting started in the right direction. I wish you all the best, my friend."

"Ladies and gentlemen," Harley's dad spoke up from the middle of the large room. "Not only are we here tonight to celebrate Harley being cleared by the celebrated and, I might add attractive, lawyer T.J. Allison." Everyone applauded. "But, we are tonight announcing the joining of two corporations, the Medler Corporation and Mid Asia Investment Corporation."

"We are joining forces in a new casino venture on the river. Hopefully, we can begin construction very soon. As president of the Medler Corporation, I know this will boost the economy of our area and we are sure this undertaking will revitalize our community."

All the room burst into applause.

Jake turned to Harley. "What do you know about this, Harley?"

"Just that the company had applied for a license, but I don't know anything about this Asian thing. Dad and granddad make all the big decisions and tell the board how to vote."

T.J. walked up to Jake and told him she needed to be going if she was going to get an early start back to Memphis the next day.

"Harley, I'm very glad things turned out well for you. I'll be speaking to you on some family matters later on."

Harley smiled and hugged her. "I don't usually hug my lawyers, but seeing how Cupid has taken over Jake when he looks at you, well that makes you a 'special lawyer'," he said with a wink and patted Jake's arm.

"You wouldn't know Cupid if he hit you between the eyes, Harley Medler!" Jake said shaking his head.

After thanking the Medlers and saying their good-byes, Jake and T.J. left the party. As they drove down the driveway Jake turned on the radio. Soft rock music from the 60's was playing. T. J. and Jake began to talk over the evening's events and the announcement.

"T.J.," Jake asked, "Was that Asian company the same company that was trying to get dirt on the Medlers?"

T.J. didn't answer right away. Finally she said, "What are you leading too, Jake?"

"Just that some of the things old Mr. Medler said to me made me think they were the same."

"As a matter of fact," T. J. replied, "they were the main competing bidders against the Medlers for the river frontage."

"Man," Jake said shaking his head, "one minute people are tying to put you in jail and the next minute they are in bed with you. This big business world is beyond me."

"It's a smart merger with the Medler's holding onto control of anything built in the area. The Medler Corporation has 51% of the holdings in this corporation, the controlling percentage. And besides, Harley was vindicated in the process!"

"Are you sure your investigator got all the information right," Jake asked.

"He wasn't exactly my investigator on this case. He was hired by the elder Mr. Medler to work for my firm and was paid by the Medlers."

"Where are we going?" T. J. asked looking around.

Jake turned the car into the cemetery and answered, "We are here."

Chapter 10

ಏ§

The car rolled to a stop and as Jake turned off the key he said, "remember at the tower the other night you asked if there were any other special places like that one. Well, this is the other special place for me."

Getting out of the car, Jake walked around and opened the door, taking her hand as she stepped out.

"I have something else to show you!"

As they strolled through the grave markers, T.J. remarked that this was something she had never done. Jake stopped and bent down indicating that they were at their destination.

He began wiping off a flat marble stone on which were written two names; Melissa and Jacob Southern, Loving Parents.

"These are my parents," Jake said looking up at T.J. and she smiled back at him. "I worked and bought this marker for them. When they died there were just two small stakes, each one with a number on it. Mother wouldn't have approved of some of the stuff that I did to get the money for the stone. It was delivered the day of my high school prom. I came out here and spent the night talking to them both about my plans for the future and all the fears I was having. Kind of silly now that I look back, I guess."

"No Jake," T.J. said softly, "it was a wonderful thing to do."

T.J. bent down beside him and put her arm around his shoulder and kissed his cheek.

Jake continued, "I had such a short time with them both, but I still keep all of those moments in my mind. To this day, I still see both their faces."

Back at the hotel parking lot T.J. and Jake stood holding each other.

"Do I still get that call you mentioned? You know - the Hawaii thing?" T.J. asked.

Stepping back Jake looked at her. "Hey, us Southern men are men of our word, and besides you would sue me if I didn't follow through as I promised. And being the good lawyer that I know you are, you would win!"

"I'd ask for six months of servitude," she said laughing.

"Doing house work and laundry, I suppose?"

"Among other things," she grinned.

Then Jake softly kissed her and as she pressed against him, it was as though she melted into him. Her body became one with his. He thought it was as if in these last few days, these brief moments, she had melted into his life, as if she had always belonged there.

She backed up, still looking into his eyes and turned and walked away.

Jake awoke the next morning to sunlight pouring through the porthole. He lay still, relishing the swaying and rocking of the boat. He could hear footsteps on the deck outside and then the sliding of the deck chair. He got up and looked outside. He saw the back of a white-haired man with large shoulders sitting in a chair looking out over the river in the morning light.

It was the Judge.

"Good morning sir," Jake said through the open porthole.

The judge turned around and smiled. "Hello son, I thought I would spend the day with you, if you don't have anything better to do. Come on out."

Jake pulled on a pair of slacks and walked out onto the deck. Early morning on the river was a beautiful sight: birds were singing, a slight mist was rising over the water, rays of sunshine gleamed off the ripples in the river. Now and then a fish would jump creating more ripples, as if to say, "Just try and catch me."

Everything seemed slow and easy, taking you far away from the cares of the world, and if you would let yourself, you would be lulled by the mighty river's hypnosis.

The judge spoke, "You have been running around like a chicken with his head cut off since you got into town. Now that the Medler boy has gotten his mess straight, I thought you might have some time for this old used-up judge."

"Della fixed us some snacks," he said motioning to a basket near his chair.

"I haven't even had my morning coffee yet, Judge."

"I almost picked up that coffee habit once back in the war, but there's something about the taste of coffee cooked in a helmet that will turn you against it," the Judge said with a big laugh.

"I've been there and done that, sir," Jake replied with a remembering smile.

They both sat looking out over the river.

"That old river is low and summer smooth," the Judge finally spoke up.

"Your dad always loved this river. In Korea there would be a lull in the fighting and all he wanted to talk about was this place and getting back to his boat and to your mom."

"You served with dad during the war sir? I didn't know that!"

"I thought you knew," exclaimed the Judge. I was the squad leader in his guard unit. I had graduated from law school and started my practice when we were called to active duty. I guess your folks thought you wouldn't be interested."

"No sir, it just never came up, that I can remember."

"Your dad should have received that medal, instead of me," the Judge continued as he settled into his chair and stared off into the past. "There were twelve of us on the side of that ridge overlooking a valley pass below. My orders were to observe any movement towards the pass by the North Koreans and hold my position. The Commies knew we were there and had sent some patrols to try to flush us out. During the night, a round went through my helmet and barely grazed my head. You know how head wounds are? That scrape bled like crazy, and by the next morning my shirt was soaked with blood."

"Your dad was my platoon sergeant, and he insisted that I go back to the command area over the hill to get it sewed up. I was getting weak, so I agreed to get the wound taken care of. When I got to the aide station some medic went to work and sewed me up. They gave me a transfusion and I must have fallen asleep, but was awakened by two guys putting me on a stretcher. They told me our company was pulling back, and that the North Koreans were overrunning everything. I was on my way to a MASH unit in the rear. I asked them if my platoon had gotten back, but neither one of them knew. While they were getting another stretcher, I removed the plasma needle and got off the jeep and headed for the commanding officers area. Everything was in a state of confusion."

"I asked the old man about my guys, and he said the last word they had from the field phone was that they were being over run, and then it had gone dead. I asked the captain for permission to check for survivors before we pulled out. I guess I looked a mess, all the dirt, dried blood, bandaged head and all. Anyway, he told me to get on a jeep and get out of there, and said something about it being too late for those guys on the ridge."

"I was thinking the hell with orders and him and looked around and saw this kid walking by with two cans of ammo. He looked real green, as if he had just arrived from the states that day. I stopped him and told him I needed him and that ammo and to come with me. I grabbed a BAR and we headed up the hill and down the other side. It seemed like it took forever. It was getting dusky dark by this time. When we got to the ridge where your dad was, there were three guys left of our squad of twelve. They were in a hole with him, and dead Koreans all around."

"I hollered his name as we approached, and he spun around and saw me. I grabbed this kid and jumped in the hole. Your dad fell back and said, 'I figured you would be back Nate!'"

"I did what I could for the boys that were wounded and sent the kid back over the hill for some help. Your dad and I took our positions and waited. I looked over at him as we talked and saw him shivering. I asked if he was okay, and he said he was."

"They started coming at us during the night, it was the longest night of my life. We both just kept firing, mostly at shadows and rifle flashes."

"Anyway, the next morning the C.O. and the kid I had sent for help came over the ridge with a bunch of guys. The kid had gotten lost during the night. Anyway, your dad and I must have looked like hell. There were North Korean bodies lying everywhere. They counted eighty something."

"The next thing I knew, while I'm recouping in the hospital, I'm told by our C.O. that he had put me in for the Congressional Medal of Honor, and your dad a silver star. I tried to explain that your dad deserved the CMH, but they didn't want to hear that. That's how I wound up this big hero. But I never forgot who the hero was."

The Judge turned and looked at Jake, "Your dad son - he was the hero!"

"Maybe you think that way Judge, but I'm sure dad was thinking you came back for him and the other guys, and in his eyes you were the hero."

The Judge nodded, "Guess you are right, it depends on your prospective. But the war changed him. He tried hard to forget and put it behind him, but it never seemed to leave him . . . nor me."

Jake spoke up, "I remember him screaming in the night and hearing my mother's voice calming him back to sleep. Now the doctors call it Post Traumatic Stress Disorder."

"Son, you know how war affects people in different ways. Well your dad and I were young and scared, but afterwards we dealt with our memories in our own different ways; the good memories, and the bad ones. It just seemed to be harder for him."

"The day I took your dad to the veteran's hospital in Jackson, he said what I thought at the time were some crazy things, about me taking care of you and your mom. I kept reassuring him that the doctors would fix him up, that he should talk to the head doctors and he would be fine. But I guess, in his mind, he had given up on bearing what is sometimes the weight of life. And then your mom grieved over the loss of Jacob. She had worked very hard, for a very long time. She let go of life too. She loved him, and consequently when she lost him, she lost her will to live."

After a long silence, the Judge pulled out a large cigar and lit it, leisurely blowing out the smoke.

"Your father lost his will to live. He took a syringe and shot air into a vein. That's what one of the doctors at the VA hospital told me. I guess he thought that death was the solitary way he could get rid of the ghost he carried with him all those years. Your dad and I stayed close after Korea, but I knew he couldn't shake his memories. I told him many times that if the facts were known, he had earned that medal. I even tried to tell General McAuthur himself, when he was hanging the thing over my neck. The Judge shook his head. "Those news people and photographers were everywhere and flashbulbs were going off. He never heard a word I said."

"The world needed heroes back in the beginning of that war. It was a better story than the death in the mud and ditches; bodies of young men being torn apart, countries trying to show the world who's got the biggest stick. But you know all of this, Jake, you of all people know about paying the price for the loss of innocence and loss of youth!"

These weren't questions the Judge was asking; it was a statement of fact. It was a fact that they both knew all too well.

He continued, "your father didn't care about being a hero and getting medals. The most important thing to him was you and your mother and your happiness, and he went a route he thought was the best for the two of you. It may possibly not have been the right thing to do in my mind, but in his, it was."

"Is ya'll done caught all da fish?" It was Jessie walking up the dock.

"Come on up Jessie, we haven't even baited a hook yet," Jake said grabbing Jessie's hand to pull him onto the deck.

"Judge, Della says you better take yo medicine. You left it at da house." Jessie handed the Judge the bottle.

"Why hell, Jessie, that stuff isn't going to do any good except for pain."

As he reached, the bottle was knocked from Jessie's hand and fell to the deck at Jake's feet. Jake bent over to pick up the plastic bottle, and read the label that said the contents were morphine. Jake handed the bottle to the Judge.

"I would be able to get more relief from that stuff Jake used to sell than this," he said as he opened the bottle, took out a pill, and swallowed it.

Afterward he settled back in his chair. Jake could tell the medicine quickly took effect as the Judge began to speak more unhurriedly and softly.

Jake reached and grabbed a chair and handed it to Jessie, who placed it on the other side of Judge Cole and sat down.

"You is got ta take care of yo self Judge, cause you is all we got."

Judge Cole looked at Jessie and smiled. "No, Jessie, it's the other way around; you and Della are all I have. Besides, our boy Jake here. He's back with us now!"

"Judge," Jessie spoke up. "When you give me dat year in jail, I knowed you was a fine man. If"n hit had been some other judge I'd a got life. I never will forget you for dat."

Jake turned to look at his two friends. "What jail time? Life for what?"

"You tell him ifin you want to, Judge."

"Years ago," the Judge began, "Della was working in the fields and two boys beat and raped her. Jessie had always been sweet on her and when he found out what had happened, he found the two boys working in a field and confronted both of them. A fight ensued; both guys jumped Jessie and he beat them to death. The case came to my court, and after I heard all the facts about the case, I sentenced him to a year in jail."

"But Judge," Jessie spoke up, "every body was a say'en you could'a give me life."

"Jessie, if I was in your position at the time, I would have done exactly what you did," the Judge continued.

"Anyway, when Della was well enough, I gave her a job and when Jessie got out of prison, Della and I went and got him and I married them. They've watched after me ever since. Guess you could say, we all lived happily ever after!"

The Judge placed his arm on Jessie's back and continued, "and I've come to love them both." The two men looked at each other and Jessie nodded his head in agreement. In that nod and look there didn't need to be words. One could tell these two men loved and admired each other.

"Boys, you are going to have to excuse me, but for some reason I have to lie down for a while," the Judge said as he rose from his chair and went inside.

"Hits dim pills. Day do him like dat," explained Jessie

"I never knew about all that jail stuff," Jake said. "I assumed you and Della had been with him forever."

"Hit sho seems that way. After dem boys did what day did, Della wasn't right, you know, fo haven babies. But dats all right wit me. I has loved dat woman since we was babies, I guess."

Jake laughed, "I know you have, and she loves you, I can tell by the way she fusses at you the most."

"Aw, you can't pay no tention to dat., Da mo she likes you, da mo she fusses!."

The two men fished and talked all morning. Later that afternoon a young man walked up to the side of the boat.

"Mr. Southern," he asked.

"Yes," Jake replied.

"There's a phone call for you at the boat store at the end of the marina."

"Thanks," Jake said, wondering who could be calling.

"Hello," Jake said as he picked up the phone.

"Jake, this is T.J. How are you?"

"Great," he replied. "How did you find me?"

"I called Judge Cole's house and Della gave me the marina's number. She said you and the Judge were spending the day together. Actually, I needed to speak to the Judge, but I couldn't pass up an opportunity to speak to you also."

"I'm glad you didn't," Jake replied. "How are things in the big city?"

"Pretty busy right now. The Meddler's have their gaming license and we've been in the process of acquiring the property along the river for the casino. I've come upon some facts you might be interested in. It seems your friend, Judge Cole, owns just about all the land the Medlers want to purchase. In the last few years he's been buying up any property that came up for sale in the town, and it appears that he's going to be the principal land owner along the river front."

"I don't understand? How could he acquire that much property? I never thought the Judge was all that wealthy, and besides, what would he want with all that land?"

"It happens sometimes, Jake. He was privy to most of the things going on and saw an opportunity to cash in on it maybe. Being the main landowner, he could just about name his own price. Judge Cole's grandfather and father were very prominent attorneys in the state, and from what information my paralegals have gathered in the state records, Judge Cole was the sole heir to a pretty substantial amount of money.

But the most surprising thing we have uncovered is this was done using the name of I.L.T.T. Corp. And this same corporation is closing a deal with Drake Power, one of the largest Power companies in the country, to build a power plant in your front yard, which is right there along the riverfront. It took quiet a bit of work to find out who and what I.L.T.T. is.

I've got to give it to him, he ran us through some legal mazes. Jake, if this deal closes, that land is worth far more than it would be to build a casino. And the value to that area in terms of jobs and growth is boundless."

Jake was quiet for a moment. "T.J., this is a big thing, wow! I know you aren't aware of this, but the fact is that Judge Cole is dying, and he doesn't have much time left."

"Oh my Jake, I'm so sorry. No, I didn't know," T.J. replied.

Next Jake continued, "The Judge is a lot of things, and I've always thought I knew people; him particularly, but greed or lust for riches is not what I've ever seen in him."

"Well Jake, you've been gone a long time and people do change!"

"Not the Judge," Jake sighed. "It just doesn't ring true with me somehow. I'll tell the Judge you called as soon as he gets up from his nap. He wasn't feeling well earlier."

"Please do Jake," T.J. said. "And I'm so very sorry. I'll be in my office until late. Anytime he wants to call me back will be fine. And I'll be in touch with you too!"

"Please do!" he said as he hung up the phone.

Chapter 11

As Jake walked to the boat, he could see Jessie baiting a hook with a worm and swinging the line over the side. Jake grabbed a cane pole and took a seat adjacent to Jessie.

"Sump'tin wrong, Jake?"

"No, I guess not, that was T.J. She wanted to speak to the Judge. Jess, do you know anything about the Judge buying up land in town?"

Jessie was looking out across the river. "You might otta ask da Judge bout it, dats his business."

"I guess you're right."

"Sides dat, I better be gett'en, cause Della's gonna be looken for me at da house fo long."

"You gonna bring da Judge home when he wakes up?"

"Sure I will."

"If he look like he hurt'in you make him take dem pills, okay?"

"No problem. I'll keep an eye on him."

As Jessie stepped off the boat onto the dock, he turned to Jake.

"Da Judge, he gonna splain everything when da time's right." Jessie turned around and walked away.

"What are you so quiet and gloomy about? Where's Jessie? Can't you get them old stubborn catfish to bite?" Jake turned to see Judge Cole coming out of the cabin door.

"Jessie had to get home. How are you feeling, sir?"

"Fine as fresh gin cotton," the Judge replied, as he ran his fingers through his thick white hair. "Did you try spitting on the hook?"

Taking a seat close to Jake, the Judge lit his cigar and leaned back. "Where did you say Jessie was?"

"Gone home, sir. He's afraid Della was going to hunt him down."

"Oh, by the way, you had a phone call from T.J. I told her you were resting and she said she would be in her office until late; to give her a call."

"Jake, that's a fine-looking, smart woman. You ought to try setting a hook in her. But more to the point, in my opinion, it's time for you to find a good woman. You don't want to wind up like me; an old bachelor 'till the end of your life."

"As I recall, sir, you were a rounder with the ladies."

"My problem, Jake, was I loved them all. In fact, too many." With a big laugh he slapped Jake on the back.

"What about you son? All the places you've been. There must have been a few dozen close calls."

"If the truth be told Sir, I was so focused on being successful in my military career that I never took the time, or possibly I was never in the right place at the right time with the right person."

"You know, I think you've hit on what I've pondered the majority of my life, Jake."

"What's that sir?"

"About being with the right person at the right time. Hand me those worms," the Judge said, as he reached for a fishing pole leaning against the railing and began unraveling the line.

"Right time, right person," the Judge quietly muttered to himself.

The two men sat back, oblivious to the towboat gradually coming up the river in front of them. They sat in silence, absorbed in their own individual thoughts, watching their corks bobbing up and down in the river and listening to the sounds of the river: water lapping against the dock, birds singing in the surrounding trees, people on the dock talking and carrying on their everyday tasks. It was a lazy summer day; a good day for reflection.

The Judge at last broke the silence, "You seem to be mighty quiet this evening, Jake. Your mind somewhere else?"

"Oh, no sir, as a matter of fact my mind is without a doubt here. Could I ask you something that is absolutely your business and not mine?"

"Well," Judge Cole said turning to face Jake, "it depends on what the question is."

"It's about the conversation I had with T.J. earlier today. Her staff was checking up on property deeds along the river and in town, and the largest part of the land is owned by a corporation called I.L.T.T., and that corporation is you!"

The Judge smiled. "It didn't take her long to find me out did it? And I thought I was clever," Judge Cole busted out into laughter. "You should see the look on your face, Jake."

"I don't understand Judge. What's it all about?"

Judge Cole pulled out a handkerchief from his back pocket and wiped his eyes. "I pulled a slick one on the Medler's son, that's what it is all about. I hope old man Medler has the same look as you do when he finds out too," and the Judge roared with laughter again.

"Oh boy," said the Judge shaking his head and again wiping his eyes.

"You've lost me somewhere, sir. What's going on?"

"Well, I'll catch you up, son. I own most of the property that the Medler Corporation is going to need along the town riverfront for their moneymaker development, and they are going to have to deal with me, or my estate, before they will be able to use it. But the shoe is on the other foot this time. Now, instead of the Medlers milking this community, this community is going to milk the Medlers."

"Because the cost of leasing the land that I own will go back to the community in the form of scholarships, town maintenance, schools, you name it. I'm giving it back to the town, all of it!" The Judge placed his hand on his chest. "There are no big fake promises now, and the folks of the community get nothing later. It's all drawn up and ironclad. Son, this part of the world has always been divided among the haves and the have-nots. If the Medlers want to go ahead with their project, they will have to do it somewhere else. I listened to the planning and the big talk about how their project was going to be good for the town, and what the people would get out of it. I could read between the lines.

Therefore, I decided to buy some insurance for the town in the form of land. . land that the Medlers would need."

"Then, low and behold, here comes a representative of this big power company with an offer to purchase the land that I'd purchased thru the years for a plant site. This is heaven-sent for my town and the folks that need jobs and industry - an answer to my prayers. The best part is that it's all in one package."

"I thought that this land along the river belonged to the town previously, that it was public property," Jake said. "How did you buy it?"

"I had access to all the old land deeds at the courthouse and discovered that a deal was struck with the original owners. The city leased the land for a river port a hundred years ago; the original owners would retain ownership and the city would maintain the property and get the taxes. That agreement expired five years ago, and no one noticed. I'd contacted the heirs and made them an offer to buy the land, at twice its value."

"I bought it all, except for one spot. It seems your friend Harley's lady friend and her relatives own that spot and they didn't even know it."

"You mean Debbie Jenkins?"

"Yes, her grandfather's name was on the deed - her father's father - and it's the key property to the whole deal. The old man must have been a rounder according to what I've read in some old county records. He won the land and a ferry business in some riverboat poker game just after the civil war. He was a hard drinker, similar to Debbie's father. Anyway, I wasn't able to talk to her or her mother."

"Sir, why didn't the Medlers go ahead and buy all this property before? That would have been the wise business move, it would seem to me."

"Greed and arrogance, son. Nearly all of the businesses along the river were folded because the bank called in loans or refused to put more money into them. And who owns the bank? The Medlers!"

"With everything along the river front closing, my guess is they felt certain they could keep control of the property, devalue it, and when the time was right, start buying the remaining land cheap. But they never figured on an old coot like me!"

Jake shook his head, "No sir I guess not. That must have taken a lot of money."

"The Cole's have been putting money away for years. I figured I would just put it where it would do the most good. I put aside enough to take care of Della and Jessie for the rest of their days, and what's more, this trip I'm due to go on doesn't require money."

"Judge Cole!"

Jake and the Judge could see Jessie walking hastily up the dock.

"Judge, da governor, he at da house. Della told him you ain't there but he say, he gonna wait till I gets you."

Standing up the judge commented, "Hell, I didn't even vote for him."

"Guess old man Medler is calling in some big favors, now that he knows about the land. Come on Jake, let's pay our respects," motioning as he stepped onto the dock.

Della was waiting at the door as the men arrived. "He in da den Judge. You wants some coffee served?"

"Why hell no, Della. That will mean he'll stay that much longer."

Opening the sliding pocket door into the study, Jake could see a graying, well- dressed, middle-aged man seated in the Judge's chair behind the large, hand-carved walnut desk.

"Judge Cole, nice to see you again," the governor said as he stood and put out his hand. Ignoring the governor's hand, Judge Cole walked around to the other side of his desk. "This old chair was hand made for this old rear end. Have a seat around the other side governor, if you will. That's Jake Southern."

The governor looked at Jake and nodded. Jake smiled.

"I need to speak to you alone, Judge, if you don't mind," the governor said looking at Jake.

"Say what you've come to say, governor. This is Jake's home too."

"Well, Judge I'm here to speak to you on behalf of the people of this county and this state."

"Cut to the chase," interrupted the Judge. "You are here on behalf of the Medlers, who were big backers for you in this part of the state." The Judge leaned back in that grand old chair.

Jake smiled to himself. He could tell the Judge was in his glory.

"What do the Medlers want you to talk me into governor?"

"Judge Cole, I'm in a position to offer you my offices full support to a seat on the State Supreme Court."

"Ain't that something, Jake?" smiled the Judge.

"And what do I do for this wonderful opportunity?" the Judge continued glaring at the man who seemed to look smaller as the conversation went on.

"The Medler Corporation is prepared to completely reimburse you for all the properties you have purchased, with, I might add, a considerable profit." The governor seemed pleased that he was regaining control of the situation and thought he had gotten the old man's attention.

"You know, boy," said the Judge as he leaned back in his chair. "Over the past, I don't care to remember how many years, I've had every variety of politician come to me; to me, a modest, old, country judge, with his butt in the air for me to kiss. And if I kissed it just right I might get a pat on the head. Well, I've never been for sale, and I'm not for sale now! You tell your big money backers that, if you would sir, and thank you for your time!"

"Come on Jake. Let's get some coffee." And with that said, the Judge rose from this chair and walked out of the room. With a wave of his hand he said to the confused governor sitting there, "You can find your way to the door, can't you governor?"

As Jake stepped aside and held the door open to the kitchen, he looked into the Judges' face and could see that the confrontation had taken more from the Judge than he had let on.

Della turned from the table and grabbed the Judge's arm as he began to stagger. With one quick motion she spun a chair around and placed it under the Judge, and he sank into the chair.

"Gimme dim pills," she said to Jessie as he came from the side of the room. Removing the pill bottle from his shirt pocket, he opened the bottle and shook out two pills. Della filled a glass of water from the sink faucet and gave it to the Judge to drink.

"Should we call the doctor?" Jake asked looking at Della.

"No, he gonna be all right. Jus let him sit for a spell. He got himself all riled up."

The Judge was shaking his head as he gulped some water and swallowed his pills. "I'm fine son, I just forget sometimes that I'm supposed to take things slower."

Jake thought that the Judge's color seemed to be returning.

"Looks like the Medlers are going to be ready to chat and get real cozy pretty soon," smiled the Judge weakly.

"I don't know what I'm gonna do wit you." Shaking her head Della took a chair in front of the Judge. "Dis stuff is gonna kill you fo yo time."

Judge Cole placed his hand on Della's. "I'm fine Della. And I'm going to last longer than that old quack doctor!"

"That old quack doctor is younger than you is," Della snapped back with a smile. They all began to laugh. "Let's have some coffee now," said Jake.

As Della was getting the coffee, the phone rang. Della picked it up, "Judge Cole's residence. Just one moment," she said and placed her hand over the mouthpiece. "Hit's Mr. Medler Sr., Judge."

Reaching for the phone, he said, "Judge Cole speaking."

Mr. Medler started, "Judge, the governor just called from his car and recommended that I speak to you directly about this property thing. I'm sure we can work something out. We've always been able to talk things out thru the years, Nate! Would you be interested in coming by my office at the bank tomorrow to discuss it?"

"Why, I'd be glad too, Harley. What time are we talking about?"

"Oh, say about 10:00 am if that fits your schedule."

"That's fine. Thanks for calling," and the Judge handed the phone back to Della.

"Well, my boy, now the ball is really rolling." The Judge looked at Jake.

"I sure hope it works out, sir." Jake took a seat across the dinner table from the Judge and lifted his coffee.

"Oh, there's no doubt that it's going to work, son. I've just got to tie up one thing, and that's the Jenkins' land. And I want you to handle it for me by making her the offer. But I think right now, I'd like to go for a ride. So Jake, my boy, would you be good enough to drive me?"

"Yes sir, I'd be glad to, but maybe you should rest first."

"No, No! I'm fine and besides how hard is it to sit and ride?"

"Well, you ain't got my blessin'," Della spoke up as she stood in the middle of her kitchen with her hands on her hips.

"Della, we'll be right back. I just need to look around for awhile," the Judge said as he looked up at her with her dark eyes fixed in a glare at the ailing man.

Jake thought to himself, as he watched the scene, that it was like a small boy getting approval to go out and play instead of practicing his piano lessons. He also thought he detected a trace of a tear in one of Della's eyes as she quickly turned away and spoke softly at the same time.

"Hit don't make no never mind to me. Ya'll get fo I get dat broom on the both of you. And Jessie you better get to da store fore it closes."

The two men settled into Jake's car. The Judge gave directions and Jake drove up the road and out of town. The highway appeared as straight as an arrow on the flat delta land. The fields on each side of the highway seemed to stretch on forever, with only a shade tree here and there and at the end of some fields, to break up what appeared to be endless crops of soybeans and cotton.

Jake had asked Uncle Ned one time, in his youth, why the farmers didn't just cut those few trees down. Uncle Ned replied, "Dat's where you sits and rest in da shade, boy!" It made sense to Jake at the time, and he thought to himself, it still does.

The Judge was looking at the passing scenes. He turned to look ahead. "Jake stop up at that old place on the left please."

Jake could see just ahead an old abandoned tenant house, grown over with kudzu vines. He slowed and turned into the weed and gravel-covered drive. Trash lay all around the house.

Before Jake could ask, Judge Cole spoke up.

"When I was about thirteen, I would walk out here every Saturday morning in the summer to see the most beautiful girl in the world!"

"She must have been very special and very beautiful. That's about a seven mile walk," said Jake. "I couldn't think about myself walking seven miles for a woman."

"Oh, she was. I never thought about it being a long way as I walked. All I could think about was to be with her, to see her, to hear her voice."

"We would sit on that old porch and talk all day, sometimes until dark, or until her Daddy would tell her to come in. Afterward I'd walk home filled with the time I'd spent with her. Her dad was a sharecropper and worked on this place 'till he died."

Silence settled over the car as the two men looked at the old, run-down house. Jake spoke up. "Whatever happened to the girl, Judge?"

"She married Jenkins, the man I shot in my court room."

Jake turned to face the Judge. "She was Rose Lee Jenkins?"

The Judge was nodding his head, still staring at the house.

"We went our separate ways after that summer. She married the Jenkins boy when she was fifteen. I continued in school and went on to college; and you know the rest. I'd hear stories about him beating her, but until that day I saw her in my court room battered and beaten down, I didn't know for sure." He sat still with a far away look in his eyes, remembering.

Jake spoke up, "I was in the court room that day. I saw her."

Looking over to Jake, the Judge continued. "I wanted to kill him from the start, but when he grabbed Twill's pen and jumped on the table to stab her, he gave me the excuse I needed. Now you understand why I can't go to Debbie Jenkins and ask to buy their land. I'm the man who killed her daddy. I could have taken her mom away from all the suffering they went through."

Jake put his hand on the Judge's arm, and said, "I'll talk to her and do whatever is possible."

Jake thought to himself, "The Judge must be going through some needless regrets - things he shouldn't feel responsible for. But we all have regrets. Maybe it's the morphine."

They sat for a while at the old farmhouse, and finally they drove unhurriedly back to the house in silence; the Judge thinking back to the past and Jake thinking about what lay ahead of them.

After arriving at the Judge's house, they went into the Judge's study and talked more about what the Judge wanted to offer the Jenkins for their land. Then Jake left determined to go straight to the Jenkins' the next morning and make the offer, to help the Judge in whatever way he could.

Chapter 12

Jake couldn't help but notice the large, shiny Lincoln that was parked next to the curb in front of the Jenkins' house. It looked out of place in the run-down neighborhood.

Jake walked up the cracked cement steps to the front door and knocked. Debbie came to the door and opened it. Looking up at Jake, she said: "Hi, Jake, come in out of the heat."

As she opened the door wider, he could see Harley seated on an old, tattered sofa. Rising from his seat and sticking out his hand, Harley greeted Jake. "Jake, you trying to get all the gals in town, you old dog?" Harley asked.

"No, I just needed to talk to Debbie and her mom about some business for the Judge."

"Well, I was on my way to the office. Are you coming by with him today?"

"Yes, I'll most likely be there."

"Well, in that case, I'll talk to you later." Harley starred down at his watch. "I've got to get going." He walked over to Debbie, kissed her, picked up his briefcase, and waved goodbye.

As he walked to the door he turned back, "Oh, yeah, your looker lawyer friend is supposed to be at the office this morning too." With a big grin on his face, he punched his finger into Jake's rib cage and closed the door.

"What can I do for you Jake?" asked Debbie. "Please sit down."

"Debbie is your mom home?"

"Yes, she's in the kitchen." Debbie rose and walked to the kitchen door. "Mama, Jake Southern wants to talk to us."

A small, frail woman walked into the room. Jake could see the hard years had taken their toll on her. She looked down as she sat in a chair across the room from Jake. She wouldn't look him in the eyes, he noticed.

"Can we get you some iced tea," she asked.

"No thank you ma'am. I'm here to talk to you and Debbie about some land. You are the lone survivors of Bo Jenkins, and his family owned the lands."

"Oh," Debbie spoke up. "That is what Harley was here about too; that old river land that his daddy wanted to buy from us. Mamma went ahead and sold it to him. She needed the $5000 and ..."

"What!" Jake exclaimed. "That's all Harley gave you was $5000 for that land?"

"Yes, he explained that it wasn't worth anything much, but he wanted to help mama and me. He said they was gonna maybe build something by the river. Why, do you want it too, Jake?"

Jake settled back onto the shabby torn sofa. He looked at both of the women, and begin to tell them about what the land was going to be used for, what the Judge was planning to do for the community.

Debbie looked at her mother.

"Mama, I'm sorry. I thought Harley was being straight with me. I just wanted to trust him."

Mrs. Jenkins looked at Debbie with sadness in her eyes.

"That's all right baby, you didn't know. And we needed whatever we could get."

"Mr. Southern," she said looking over to Jake, "how much could we have made selling the land to the Judge? I was just wondering."

Jake tightened his lips, then looking at her pulled out a check.

"Tell you what I'm going to do. I'm going to swap the check you have for this one." He handed her the check.

She took the check and holding it in both hands, held it out away from her as if to get it into focus. "Lord, oh Lord, is this - is this two hundred fifty thousand dollars?"

"Yes ma'am."

Debbie snatched the check from her mother's hand.

Looking at it, she stood and placed one hand over her mouth.

"Oh, Mama, Oh, Mama! But, but we signed the contract and gave it to Harley." Both women looked at Jake skeptically.

"I'm going over to take care of that little matter now if it's all right with you. If you'll sign this contract with the Judge, I'll return the check Harley gave you."

Mrs. Jenkins opened a bible on the end table and turned the pages to the slip of paper they had signed with Harley. She handed the contract and check to Jake. She then signed the contract for the Judge.

"Is this legal, what you are doing Jake?" Debbie asked.

"I promise you, when I get through, it will be. I've got to run now, but I'll call you later."

He turned and looked back at Mrs. Jenkins. "The Judge still remembers those summer visits at your house when you were kids."

She smiled and looked down. "I ain't never forgot it neither. It was a nice part of my life."

Jake left the two women, and as he got into the car and began to drive toward the bank, he kept telling himself, "Be cool, calm down."

Reaching the town square, Jake parked the car and got out. He saw Jessie pull into a parking spot in front of the bank. Jake waited for a pickup truck to pass before crossing the street to meet Jessie and the Judge.

Judge Cole got out of the passenger side. He was the first to see Jake walking up.

"You get the contract signed, son?"

"Yes sir," Jake replied. "This is it," handing the paper to Judge Cole.

"Good, let's get in and do this thing. You stick with me. You too, Jessie."

"Judge," Jake stopped him by holding his arm, "I need a few minutes with Harley before the meeting. If you will stall for a few minutes it will sure help. I'll be right in."

"Well, what in the world for? We've got everything covered."

"Yes sir, we do. I only want to discuss a few points with Harley first."

"All right. But don't be too long."

"No sir, I won't be."

Jake looked over at Jessie. "Come with me Jessie."

The three men walked into the bank lobby and up to the information desk. The elder Mr. Medler called from across the room, "Judge, come on in." The Judge walked toward Mr. Medler. Jake turned to the lady behind the information desk, "Is Harley III in his office?"

Looking to her left, she said, "Oh, yes, just knock on the door and go on in." Jake nodded his thanks, and he and Jessie walked toward Harley's door.

Jake nodded to Jessie to stand by the door. He knocked and opened the door at the same time. Harley was seated at his desk.

"Jake!" Harley said looking up. "You going to be in the meeting with Judge Cole?"

"You gave Mrs. Jenkins $5000 for that property Harley - land you know is worth far more than that. You took advantage of someone who was learning to trust you - possibly even love you!"

"You don't understand Jake, this is business! My family's business. This is my," he said pointing a finger at himself, "business! My dad needs that property and I am giving it to him. I'm showing my dad and granddad that I can contribute to our company."

"Oh, I understand Harley. I understand when powerful, unethical people step on weaker people to get what they want - and will step on anyone who gets in the way of what they want! But I wouldn't have believed you would be that way. You slithered back into a relationship with Debbie to get that piece of property – just a piece of property Harley - didn't you?"

"Well," Harley said settling back into his plush leather chair, "times change, people change." The two men looked at each other. Harley rose from his chair. "We better be getting to the meeting." Jake stepped in front of him and stood still.

"What are you doing, Jake?"

"I'm getting the contract Mrs. Jenkins signed from you and returning your check. Taking the check from his shirt pocket, he threw it on Harley's desk. Harley exclaimed, "No way! This is none of your business!"

Jake's huge hand was around Harley's throat in a flash. He pushed Harley against the wall that was covered with bookshelves. Harley managed to give out a faint yell, but Jake only tightened his grip on his old friend's throat. Harley reached up for Jake's powerful arm to get some relief, but Jake's grip only got stronger as Jake spoke slowly and calmly.

"Harley, it won't be long before you start seeing black, then not long after that the blood flow to your brain will be completely gone, and you will die. This all depends on how much pressure I apply. You see, Harley, I've spent the last twenty years in the business of killing people, so I do understand business and pressures. Now we are going to tear up that contract, are we not?"

Harley's face grimaced as he nodded agreement.

Little by little, Jake released his grip, and Harley collapsed into his chair clutching his throat. "You could have killed me, Jake!" he choked out.

Taking a seat on the corner of the desk, Jake pointed his finger at Harley. "I want the contract Harley!"

Harley pointed to a red folder on his desk. Jake opened the folder and took out the contract that had Mrs. Jenkins' signature and handed it to Harley.

"Tear it up!"

Harley took the paper, never taking his eyes off of Jake, and began tearing it into strips.

Jake rose slowly from the desk and calmly walked to the door. He stopped and faced Harley.

"When we were young, Harley, you weren't the person you are today. I thought you were still the same, but I was wrong. You have become your father and your grandfather, except it's not greed that drives you. This is just a big game and money is how you keep score. People's lives, this community - those things don't mean squat to you. Maybe that's a sign of our generation, who knows? I know that I have lost a friend!" He turned and opened the door.

Jessie was there, waiting for Jake and the two men walked together into the main lobby.

"You okay Jake?"

"Yes Jessie, I'm fine" Jake replied, looking into the big man's face. "Let's find the Judge."

Chapter 13

ॐ

The two men walked across the bank lobby and into the conference room where Jake's eyes caught sight of T.J. She was seated behind a pile of papers on the long conference table. She was bent over reading but looked up and smiled at Jake.

"Jake, glad you could come. Maybe you can help us talk some sense into this old legal eagle. You know everyone?" said Mr. Medler, Sr.

"Yes sir," Jake scanned the room briefly nodding at Miss Anna. She had her head held high and wouldn't make eye contact he noticed.

Judge Cole was seated across from Medler Jr. Jake took a seat near the Judge and Jessie sat beside Jake.

Harley came through the conference room door holding his throat with one hand. Old Mr. Medler asked Harley, "You all right, you look flush?"

Miss Ann noticed the bruising on Harley's throat. "What happened to your throat my dear?"

Harley croaked out, "sore throat" and took a seat by his father, all the while looking down. Harley leaned over to his father and whispered into his ear. Mr. Medler Jr. leaned back in his chair and looked startled into Harley's face.

Judge Cole spoke up, "You boys need to have this fine lawyer look over these papers." He stood and handed a folder to T.J.

"Okay, okay," Mr. Medler Sr. spoke up. "But let's get to the meat, Nate. What's in this for you? What's your price?"

The Judge settled back into his seat. "Harley, I want you to do well, make plenty of money. In addition, I want this town to do just as well as the Medlers."

"Nate, you have known our plans all along. You know we plan to take care of this community."

"Yes," the Judge spoke up. "I'm sure you do."

"Now, Nate! We understand the land we need is owned by you, all of it! We are prepared to pay double what you paid for your trouble."

Jake looked beside him at the Judge who was smiling.

"It's not for sale; or for lease. Your attorney I'm sure has all the information by now. There is no sense taking up any more of your time, gentlemen." The Judge rose from his chair.

"She'll explain what's been going on. Thank you for your time gentlemen. Sorry but we couldn't do business!"

"Jake, Jessie, are you ready to go?"

The two men rose from their seats and followed the Judge out of the room, leaving the three Medler men, Miss Anna and T.J. sitting astonished.

Walking down the front steps of the bank building, Jake, Jessie and the Judge were met by the sheriff and Twill.

"Good morning, Judge Cole," Twill stopped and spoke.

"What's going on Mr. Twill? Sheriff how are you?" The sheriff nodded.

"It appears we have enough evidence to arrest Mrs. Anna Medler, Judge", Twill squeaked out with enthusiasm.

"On what charges?

"Conspiracy to murder and accessory to murder!" Twill continued on, so caught up in himself and the moment he could hardly contain himself. He seemed to almost want to jump up and down with delight.

"The two involved in the fight at Lilly's with Harley Medler III were both ex-cons. It seems Mrs. Medler hired them to get rid of her son's lover. She must have tried everything through the years to stop the relationship, but had failed. So she decided on drastic measures. And the illegitimate son was going to be next!

The one ex-con we have in custody is singing like a song bird to get a lesser charge. Most likely Harley saved his girlfriend's life that night. With the one guy getting shot everything unraveled. Little did Mrs. Medler know that while she was making the deal, one of the ex-cons was recording everything she said. We have the recording. The deal was made in the parking lot of the local truck stop. The owner, Miss Dianne, saw the three talking. She remembered thinking at the time it was odd for Mrs. Medler to be at the truck stop, and especially odd for a lady like her to be talking with two men who looked so shady.

Then it gets even more crazy. Some Asian gentleman had also hired these same two guys to find some dirt on anyone in the Medler family. We're not sure why right now, but that may have been the reason for the tape recording. Maybe they were going to blackmail the Medler's. We'll find everything out I'm sure. And they won't be able to get out of this one.

We have an arrest warrant from Judge Wilson for Mrs. Medler. And we're having the sheriff in Bovine County bring the ex-con here where he will be charged as well."

Looking at Jake, Twill stood straight with his shoulders back, "Mrs. Medler's going to jail; most likely for some time." Twill turned around and proceeded to the bank door behind the sheriff.

Jake looked back at Twill as he walked away. "I'm sorry, but I just never liked that man."

The Judge laughed. "Twill's ambition isn't to be liked. He wants to move on up in the world. But where, God only knows! He's on a mission."

The three men walked down the bank steps and toward their cars. As the Judge started to get in the car, he turned and yelled to Jake, "You coming up to the house, son? Della said to remind you she's cooking her famous blackberry cobbler that you love."

"I'll be right on up!"

Jake watched the Judge and Jessie as they pulled away from the bank. The Judge was smiling. Jake stepped aside as a television station van pulled into the now vacant parking spot. The driver and passenger leaped out, one had a TV camera on his shoulder, the other with a microphone.

"Twill's at it again," Jake thought to himself. Looking up and down the street as he began to walk across to his car, he noticed a bench located underneath a large pink crape myrtle.

Jake took a seat in order to watch the scene going on across the street at the bank. "What a hot, draining day. The humidity must be 120°," Jake thought to himself.

Moments later Twill walked out the front door of the bank, followed by Miss Anna who now had both hands behind her back. The sheriff followed close behind. Twill stepped up to the camera as the other newsman began talking into a microphone. The camera man followed Miss Anna and the sheriff, whose hand was now on her arm. One of the reporters shouted out, "Mrs. Medler, how do you think this is going to affect your standing in the community?" Mrs. Medler looked up for a moment and stared directly across the street at Jake. Their eyes met for an instant, and Jake could sense her shame, or was it hate? She quickly jerked her eyes away and raised her chin.

Jake thought to himself, "was it shame he saw in her eyes? Shame that she had lost her respectability, or shame that she had lowered herself to the white trash status she had for so long detested? Was it shame at all? Or was it arrogance that she, in her position, would ever be touched by scandal? That seemed more likely to him, knowing Miss Anna."

"The webs we weave for ourselves," Jake thought, getting up from the bench as he walked to his car.

"Jake!" He turned to see T.J. coming across the street. As she walked up to him she said, "Have you got room for a friend?"

Jake looked at her. Her long, soft, red hair was in her eyes and she took one hand and pulled it away from her face. "I need a friend right now!"

Jake walked around to the passenger side of the car and opened the door.

"Aren't you afraid you'll get shot for fraternizing with the enemy?" he said looking down at her as he held the door open.

"I informed the Medlers that they would be receiving my final bill and resignation, besides I couldn't think of a better reason to be shot," she said as she smiled.

"What brought you to that decision?"

"Decided I was working for the wrong side!"

"Where to madame?"

"It doesn't make much difference. It seems I'm out of a big client in these parts."

"Your friend's mother is in big trouble." T.J. turned to face Jake as she spoke.

Before she could go any further with her story, Jake spoke up, "Yea, Mr. Twill and the Sheriff explained it to us as we were coming out of the bank."

"Those were some heavy charges. Do you think they'll stick?"

"I don't know. It may be difficult for even the Medlers to buy their way out of this."

"They were taking her to the courthouse to formally charge her. Her husband is going over later to bail her out, and he seemed quiet angry at Harley about some land deal he was supposed to have come up with. I had words with the Medlers about the plans Judge Cole has made. Bless the Judge's heart, he knew just what he was doing and how to do it. From what little I saw, it looks iron-clad. What was kinda strange is that he did all this land dealing for all these years without knowing about this power plant coming in. And from what I understand all the proceeds go back into the town. There aren't a lot of people like that these days! He is one-of-a-kind."

"Maybe not one-of-a-kind," Jake answered, "but definitely rare, I'd say."

Jake continued to drive down Main Street until he crested the top of the levee overlooking the river. He pulled over on top and came to a stop. The marina was below and to the south, a gray storm cloud could be seen.

"Looks like we may get another shower to cool things off," he spoke up.

"Good! This humidity is killing my hair."

T.J. placed her hand on the side of her hair and pulled it back. She turned to Jake and took his hand and looked straight into his eyes.

"I've thought of nothing else but your offer to go fishing," she laughed.

Jake could feel his face flush.

"T.J.," he spoke, "I'm not a big bull shooter when it comes to anything. I want to spend time with you, and I thought at the time I asked that would be a great opportunity to do just that."

"Hush," she said as she placed her finger to his lips. She thought to herself, he's so much like a little boy. "I understand. But I've got a better idea. How about us spending the rest of the summer on that wonderful old boat of yours? You can teach me how to catfish! And besides, I think you may need to stay around here awhile."

Looking into her soft blue eyes Jake said, "And T. J. Allison, what are your intentions?"

"To catch a big catfish," she smiled.

Jake pulled her tenderly to him and kissed her. After that they stood for a long while and watched the storm clouds drift slowly up the river. It was peaceful and calming just standing there on the levee, the two of them, arm in arm, watching the river and the clouds.

"We had better get in the car and move on before the rain catches us."

They drove up the long drive to the Judge's house as it began to drizzle. Pulling up to the tall steps, Jake stopped the car. He got out and ran to the other side to open T.J.'s door, then taking her by the arm, they ran up the steps together.

The huge screen door opened and the Judge stepped out to greet them.

"Della, oh Della, bring some towels for Jake and T.J."

"Sit," said the Judge, as he fell down into his large cushioned rocker.

He held a large cigar in one hand and a glass of what the Judge called "libation" in the other.

Jessie came running up the steps with a young black boy behind him. Jake recognized him as the young boy from Uncle Ned's funeral.

Della came out of the screen door with her arms full of soft white thick towels and began handing them to each of the rain-drenched crew.

"Ya'll sit right down and dry off cause you ain't gitten my flo wet after I done got everyth'in clean."

She went back into the house and the screen door slapped shut.

A clap of thunder roared through the sky, and it began to rain harder. Everyone took a seat and watched the falling rain. Jake thought to himself about the smell that comes at the start of a summer's rain as it sweeps away the heat and beats down on the summer dust. It's one of those smells that stays with you, like the smell of fresh-baked bread. You always keep it in your senses. It always lingers somewhere in you memory.

Jessie spoke first. "Judge we is gonna have to git one of dem rid'en mowers. Dat old thang we got is on hits last leg."

"I'll call the hardware store in the morning, Jessie. You and Bobby can pick it up when you're in town."

"You working for the Judge now, Bobby?" Jake asked.

"Yea, Miss Della offered me the job to help Mr. Jessie. She said he's getting too old to do stuff around here by himself."

Jake could see that Jessie was smiling. As Jake looked at the two he couldn't help but think of his boyhood. "It starts all over again," he thought.

The screen door opened, and Della stepped out. This time she held a tray in her hands. On the tray was a large, clear pitcher filled with ice-cold lemonade and glasses for everyone. She walked over to the small table by the Judge's chair, and the door slammed shut behind her. Della set the tray down and began to pour. The tinkling of ice made everyone ready for the cold, wonderful liquid.

"Ya'll drink dis up while I finish's up da cook'en."

She stood up, putting one hand to her back.

"Lord, hit's sho is comen down."

Jessie said, "We needed dis, hits done been so…. hot."

Della walked to the screen door and opened it. She paused and turned, looking directly into Jake's eyes.

"Ain't it jus like da Lord? He sends us just what we needs - just when we needs it!"

Della smiled that full, loving smile, as her dark eyes twinkled, then closed the door behind her.

Jake took a drink and thought about that son of Debbie's.

"Wonder how he did in school and wonder what he would think of West Point?"

Printed in the United States
95442LV00002B/616-666/A